The Balloon in the Storm (and Other Conversations with Myself)

Alan J. Chambers

The Balloon in the Storm

Copyright © 2018 Alan J. Chambers

All rights reserved.

ISBN: 1-949659-02-X
ISBN-13: 978-1-949659-02-3

DEDICATION

This book is first and foremost dedicated to every teacher who encouraged me to shoot for the stars. Without them I wouldn't be where I am today.

I want to dedicate this book to my entire family.
I wouldn't trade the trials and tribulations
we've faced together with anyone else.
Thank you for sharing your time and your worlds with me.
All of you have made it hard for me to leave home,
but you make it more amazing whenever I do go back!
I love you all.

A special dedication to my little C-Ster,
Thank you for pushing me to publish this book.

My last dedication for this book is to the Swisher/Lujan family.
Thank you for letting me be a part of your family in high school,
while mine was struggling.
Thank you, Mary Swisher, for treating me like one of your own,
at the times when I didn't feel like I had anyone else to guide me.
That saved me and my future.
I am forever grateful for you buying me a bed in college,
my dreams may have crumbled with nowhere to rest them!

CONTENTS

Acknowledgments	i.
The Balloon in My Storm	1-20
Book I The Balloon	21-70
Book II The Storm	71-114
book iii other conversations with myself	115-202
i. a brighter morning	117-124
ii. born mute/locks on the door	125-140
iii. a rose	141-156
iv. born poor/shackles on the floor	157-170
v. a different flower	171-192
vi. a home	193-202

ACKNOWLEDGMENTS

Thank you to my older brother, Gabriel, for bringing the art
in my head for this book, to life with his hands.

Thank you to one of my best friends, Ethan 'Oliver',
for walking with me on this book-writing journey.
At least now that it's done I won't keep bugging him online
to check his messages to read my stories.

Thank you to my cousin Yvette, a professor of English, for taking on the
full editing project- she is brilliant! I could not have done this without her!

Thank you to my business mentors, in particular
Ebony Wyatt, Mike Maddox, and Jennifer Schneider.
Ebony for walking up to a terrified 21-year-old at one of his first big work
conferences and being a friendly face. I've appreciated the advice and
inspiration you've given me since I started my career.
Mike for letting me share my background
and then empowering me to release this dream of mine.
And Jennifer for walking me through planning my first trip
out of the United States!
My experience in Portugal had taught me how to relax.

THE BALLOON IN MY STORM

I was born mute.

I was born poor.

I will not be defined by either of those words
when the story of my life is complete.

The Balloon in The Storm is a book about perseverance.

My hope for this book is that it inspires you.

Whatever storm is going on in your life,
I'm going to ask you to look for your balloon,
something that will guide you through your storm.

Once you find it,
do not stop chasing after that balloon
until you are out of your storm.

Before you jump deeper into my book though,
I want to explain the context of my stories.

———

I was a curious case: from the time I was a toddler, I faced two separate but exacerbating disorders, Motor Skills Disorder and Oral Motor Apraxia. These affected my ability to do very simple tasks, such as hold a pencil, eat, and—most devastating to me—talk! My strength issues were caused by the Motor Skills Disorder, while my speech problems were a form of Oral Motor Apraxia. The latter causes messages of speech from the brain to not register with the mouth. The brain struggles to tell the jaw, the lips, or the tongue to move. In my situation, I had muscles that didn't work very well and brain messages that couldn't tell the mouth muscles how to move. This required me, from the age of two, to attend physical and speech therapy sessions to build up all of my muscles.

Nothing was easy for me as a small child. When I wanted to physically compete with others, I was never as strong as the children my age. When I was hungry, I struggled to eat because my mouth wasn't capable of chewing most food textures. And when I wanted to express myself, few could hear or understand me. The words that came out were too quiet, and too much of a jumbled mush. It took a lot of time for most people to make out what I was saying. I was always on the brink of tears: no one could hear me drowning in the letters that were so much easier for everyone else to swim through.

What started as a physical muteness became a lock, one blocking me out from the rest of the world. Every social situation felt like I was trapped behind a door, left to peek through the keyhole while everyone else lived on the other end. I struggled to connect with others because of my physical limitations. The amount of physical energy it took for me to speak words made it feel pointless for me to even try talking because no one could understand me anyway.

So, I began building big plans for myself and my life in the silence behind the keyhole. My childhood plans and aspirations were my balloon. When I was young, I always marveled when someone would release balloons into the sky. The horde of balloons would always rise whether it was a bright, sunny day or one filled with gloomy clouds. I'd wonder if I could be like that— able to rise despite the troubles in my life. The ideas in my head would swirl into a shape that resembled a bright red balloon, inside of which I had a vision of the life I wanted. I saw an older me in the balloon: I always pictured myself with professional attire, traveling around the world, trying exotic foods and captured in engaging conversations with friends and strangers alike. But the most important thing to me in every vision was that I always saw a man whose voice was heard. I wanted that balloon more than anything else in the world to lift me away from everything I was facing. This created my initial drive to always continue forward through any storm. I had to make the vision in the balloon real. I began to follow the balloon through my path in life—it became a friendly figure that followed me throughout my teenage years. I learned early on that failure would be a well-known acquaintance in my life; sometimes it seemed like he was the only one who would visit me behind the door I was locked behind. But I was never willing to quit. My balloon was there to guide me on my path.

I quickly grew accustomed to hard work. At only two-years-old, I had regular physical therapy sessions. These consisted of seemingly simple tasks, such as picking up sticks and stretching my hands out as far as I could while they were restrained by rubber bands. But for me, these exercises were anything but easy. I spent a little over two years building muscles and getting stronger with these little feats.

However, I was pulled out of physical therapy a bit too soon because the program I was involved in was no longer available to me. This meant any further progress to my physique would have to be achieved by other means. Luckily, my mom, who was an avid dancer herself, enrolled me in Spanish dancing, and I joined a dance group known as Los Tapatios that focused on traditional Mexican, and New Mexican dance styles. When I began, I never felt truly comfortable with the way my body was being asked to move, but, with practice and the guidance of the group's instructor, I was able to improve with each session.

Through multiple hours of practice, my cultural identity was beginning to form as well. The words and guitar strums of my ancestors playing through the dance room speakers not only helped my body form into various positions, but they also filled my spirit with my Mexican identity as the instructor guided all her tiny dancers across the floor. Though I was not a fluent Spanish-speaker at a young age, I still enjoyed hearing the stories in class and while visiting with family, and later learning what the words meant. Some of the different inflections and phonetics of the Spanish language were outside of my vocal capacity, but that couldn't stop me from representing my culture.

As my dancing ability grew stronger, I was able to perform across my hometown of Albuquerque with Los Tapatios. When we were onstage, no one's face had a bigger smile than mine, because I knew that even without words everyone understood the pride I had as I moved across the stage. Throughout my time as a dancer I was proving to myself that I could do anything the other kids could do—sometimes it just took a little longer for me to get there.

I continued to find ways to push my body as I grew older: running, lifting, and any small exercises I could find to help build me up. I kept training harder and harder every day, and by high school I was able to compete in multiple sports and I even played rugby my freshman year of college. (Caveat: I was never really good! But I always enjoyed knowing that I could at least be competitive when I tried, which is something I thought I'd never be able to do.)

Speech therapy was much more emotionally strenuous. I was in speech therapy from the ages of two through ten. However, I had to stop attending for financial reasons. The end of my speech therapy was not marked by my overall progress but by a divorce that forced me to switch schools shortly after the start of 5th grade. My mother was a stay-at-home mom prior to the divorce so when my parents split and my mother took custody of her three children (including me, my older brother Gabriel, and my younger sister Alycia) money was beyond tight as she jumped back into the workforce. I feared being a burden to an already strenuous situation, so I didn't ask to finish out my 5th grade year at the same school, and I was transferred closer to the mobile home complex we moved too. My new school didn't offer the same speech therapy services and I would have to learn to do without.

Though I had improved and had begun to open the door to the outside world, I still had issues. But because I could no longer attend speech therapy, I had to become my own teacher to fix things. There was the slight stutter that developed from being tasked with speaking slowly so as to enunciate all my words. There was also my tendency to misplace words within sentences as I was speaking. For example, instead of saying "the house is clean," my mouth would say "the clean is house." The words in my head were saying the first sentence but my mouth couldn't always follow along.

The biggest help with teaching myself came through music. My love for music began at an early age as some of my fondest memories are of joining my dad while he ran errands across the city. I never knew nor asked where we were going, I just wanted to share in learning about my dad's culture, different from the Mexican culture my mother shared with me through dance, with our mutual love of music. My dad is African-American, and his favorite genre has long been 80s and 90s R&B. Tracks by Montell Jordan, Bell Biv DeVoe, and the legendary Boys II Men were always playing when we were together. To me these musicians were the epitome of what it meant to be "cool" and "confident" for black men. The swagger they had in their voices and with the attire they wore painted a picture to me of how black men were supposed to be. I wanted to be just like them and felt like they were the archetypes of who I was supposed to become when I got older.

However, as I grew more conscious of my impediments I feared that I wasn't black enough, and it made me start to feel disconnected from my father's music. Other students started calling me an Oreo by middle school— black on the outside and white on the inside. This was particularly due to my dedication to school and the fact that years of speech therapy made my pronunciation of words sound very proper—that is, when I actually spoke aloud. Thus, I was not 'black enough' (or even Latino enough) in the other kids' eyes. I already had the ability to speak like everyone else taken from me— now my identity was being held hostage at school.

As the other students continued to convince me that I wasn't black enough, I started to find other music, that focused more on feeling alone, struggling to fit in, and being an outcast. My interests shifted from my dad's 90s R&B to more contemporary rock, and I began to study everything that I was listening to. My playlists began filling up with bands like Brand New, Jimmy Eat World, and blink-182. With lyrics like "So, it's sad this doesn't suit you now. And me fresh out of rope... Please ignore the lisp, I never meant to sound like this"[1] and "I'm ripe with things to say, the words rot and fall away. If this stupid poem could fix this home, I'd read it every day,"[2] I felt understood. Finally the issues I faced at home as well as with my speech were reflected in the music I was listening to. I would spend hours looking at the lyrics of songs, memorizing them, and singing along. I started to notice that when I did this I had complete control over my voice: the usual quirks and trembles seemed to disappear when I knew exactly what to say. And because of this, singing made me feel on top of the world.

  In 6th grade I began to write my own lyrics and found that I was writing content closer to the rock music I had discovered. As a young boy with a skin tone close to a light caramel, I felt a bit out of place, as most of the people who either listened to or played in the bands I was listening to didn't look like me. At times, I felt like I had to lead a double life, hiding my music from some friends to avoid being judged for not listening to 'black' music.

  Then I found the band Sum 41, who spoke to me on multiple levels. First, there was the fact that members of the group rapped verses in some tracks. I fell in love with their ability to infuse a genre I grew up with into the new one I was growing to appreciate. Second, in addition to their music, the lead guitarist of Sum 41 went by the moniker of Dave "Brownsound" Baksh (a moniker that I attempted to claim through middle school). Though Dave Baksh was of Indo-Guyanese descent, for

---

[1] Brand New, "The No Seatbelt Song" (2001)
[2] Blink 182, Stay Together For The Kids" (2001)

the first time I saw someone who looked more like me in one of my favorite bands.

After reaching out to Baksh on MySpace and receiving an encouraging response back, I signed up for guitar classes at the start of middle school and begun to play. The lessons had me start with the basics and required intricate finger work that I struggled with as we were taught exercises to help us stretch our fingers to play more complex pieces in the future. My hands would frequently cramp by the end of guitar class, making the rest of the school day miserable as holding and writing with a pencil after the lessons was a painful task for me. However, I persevered through the lessons and hand cramps and became proficient at the guitar by the 8th grade. At that point, I had purchased my own guitar and would figure out ways to blend the lyrics I was writing with the chords I was now able to play. I would spend many middle school nights getting lost between the sweet sound of nickel and bronze guitar strings and my own voice singing to the words I wrote.

Still, I remained terrified by the idea of singing my music in front of everyone, too worried about my stutter slipping out or my music not fitting the status quo. That was until I found a mixtape that would change my life. *A Kid Named Cudi (2008)* was the first work released by Kid Cudi, and it forever altered my relationship with hip-hop. Finally, I found an album that stretched across genres and touched on topics that made me feel like it was okay to be black and emotional. In my favorite track, "Man on the Moon," Kid Cudi states: "Close my eyes, hide in the dark. <u>It's a curtain call; come one, come all</u>. <u>All I do is try to make it simple</u>. The ones that make it complicated. Never get congratulated. I'm something different, all aspects." When I heard these words, it felt like Cudi *got* me. I found a rapper who, like me, felt misunderstood, someone who felt disconnected enough to be a man on the moon. I started to find myself delving back into hip-hop, finding mixtapes and albums of similar artists such as **POS, Wale, Charles Hamilton, 88 Keys,** and **Kanye West** (especially his 2008 album *808s & Heartbreaks*). My new-found love for hip-hop began to influence my own music as I tried to find ways to add hip-hop influenced guitar riffs to my rock songs as well as producing hip-hop tracks under the moniker Quietbeats.

Slowly, I began to allow myself to sing for others to hear through high school. I started a band that got to play a few shows. I participated in my high school choir and learned how to hone my craft; I even created a mixtape letting some friends rap over the tracks while I would sing the hooks.

In retrospect, I've come to realize that the hours I spent practicing were a form of speech therapy, building up the muscles needed to speak fluently. Music had given me my voice. I may always be more of a quiet man because it is so ingrained in my nature to have a quiet disposition, but I've found my ability to speak strong enough, and loud enough so that others will listen.

While working through those physical challenges my family had many struggles as well. We struggled financially, to the point of not always knowing where we would be sleeping at night. Amidst my parents' divorce came the foreclosure of our house. My father at this point had been working as a manufacturing technician at the local General Mills plant. The job was enough to lift us to a lower-middle to middle income family, but the marriage turned sour and anger would linger throughout the household waiting to ravage my parents' finances. I would hide in my room with pillows over my head when the fights became too much for me. At the end of their relationship my parents couldn't agree on any basics, which led to no one making payments on the house. We lived at the top of our cul-de-sac and on an early fall afternoon during my 5th grade year, my brother and I walked up the street after school when I noticed the orange piece of paper hanging on the front door. I remained calm as my brother explained what 'Foreclosure' meant to me. All that I understood was that my bed was no longer mine. I resisted the urge to cry as the rest of the day turned into a blur. One of our parents would pick us up and explain the situation. All I thought about after that was that my balloon would get me out of this storm. Following the foreclosure, my parents' finances were destroyed as they both had to file for bankruptcy. The next two months became a blurry revolving door of the couches and floors of strangers and other family members.

Eventually my mother found a mobile home and moved myself and my siblings in with her. Everything changed for all of us as the sense of safety and comfort afforded to us in our previous household was in stark contrast to the discomfort I felt in the mobile home. The mobile home was previously occupied by a landlord who was a cat owner and the mobile home felt very much like cats were the only inhabitants. Residual kitty litter, cat hair, and urine filled the tiny home. I made a game in the room I shared with my older brother by placing towels or clothes on the ground to avoid stepping on the mobile home's carpet. My senses felt like they were on overdrive and school became an escape from the house.

As my mother's credit improved we were able to move out of that mobile home and into an apartment, and life began to feel a bit more normal by the end of middle school. My mother grinded by climbing her way out of poverty by starting to work as a receptionist at a doctor's office. Through hard work and maneuvering her career around she became a general manager at an eye glass shop. The process took her nearly four years to rise to that position. When she did, though, it allowed her to ease the burden of bankruptcy and go from renting to owning her own stationary home once she began her career as a general manager. Seeing my mother grind helped inspire me to do the same in school, I felt like if I was as dedicated to school I would be able to elevate myself in the future.

But just as it began to feel like everything was finally going to settle down in our new home, life had other plans that would not let our family breathe for long.

In the early September of my sophomore year of high school, my mother came down with a terrible cold that wouldn't go away. She went to the doctor, who then diagnosed her with Wegener's Granulomatosis, an immune deficiency disorder in which a person's body is unable to fight against most diseases. For example, if someone around you has a cold, that cold can turn into pneumonia in your body. And this is exactly what happened to my mother.

My siblings and I hadn't seen her for two weeks after she first went to the hospital, though she kept us updated on her status when she had a chance. When we finally saw her, there was talk of my aunt who lived out of state coming to say goodbye—I hadn't realized the disease was that serious. We were allowed to see my mother, and it was the first time I'd ever cried in a public setting. The strong woman who had fought for us to have a home was left looking like a shell of herself, her face in a frailed daze, unsure of where she was. I don't think she even knew that we were in the room with her. I had to leave after a few minutes because my heart couldn't take it.

She kept fighting though. The day she was expected to die had passed and we all felt relief. We were still uncertain as to whether things were going to get better or not, but we prayed that she would recover. In the following days, we received updates on her health and all indications were that she was becoming more stable. News like this continued to come week after week. The doctors had finally concluded that the worst had passed and gave the family a date that she would be allowed to leave the hospital.

In mid-to-late October, she was cleared to leave the hospital but needed a caretaker. Our grandparents took her in. My grandmother prepared her meals and helped her figure out the large assortment of pills the hospital gave my mom to maintain her health. My brother had graduated from high school a year earlier and was trying to figure out what he was going to do with his life, while my sister was starting her eighth-grade year. My siblings and I continued to live independently at my mom's house while our grandparents helped keep the utilities running and food in the refrigerator so that we could focus on school and maintain a "normal" life. Each of us would take time to go spend time with our mother at our grandparents'. But with the medication she was on, communication was minimal.

For Christmas that year we got our mother back. Though my heart felt lighter, life didn't get easier with her return. My brother would shortly leave for Texas and my sister found herself living between different houses. I had to become the new caretaker of my mom and our home. I became the 'Mother' of the house. This was difficult as a sophomore in high-school who dreamed of overcoming the odds and becoming the next big name in football. I had to adjust that dream: I needed to learn how to be a parent to my parent with what felt like no one guiding me. I learned how to clean every part of the house. I learned how to grocery shop on a tight budget to make sure whoever was staying in that home could eat. I learned how to stop crying as I tended to my mother's needs, sorting through her medication and preparing her meals. While my friends were out making memories, I was inside my house trying to sew everything together so our lives wouldn't completely unravel.

I focused on three main things: my mother's health, keeping that house as together as a fifteen-year-old boy could, and my education. My schoolwork became an escape from the reality of what my life was. I would get lost in all the projects that were assigned to me, researching intricate details of whatever topic I was assigned in order to go the extra mile. It didn't matter the subject as every second spent looking down at an assignment meant a second I didn't have to think about everything happening around me.

There was one English assignment where I was tasked with writing a personal essay on something that bothered me. I shared the state of my home life and was sent to the guidance counselor the next morning. The counselor wanted to make sure I was okay, but I didn't have the luxury to worry about whether I was okay. It wouldn't change the reality of what I was going home to. I lied to the guidance counselor that I was 'fine', and I never discussed my home life with any other teachers. I had to be strong, and I was scared that addressing in conversation what was going on in my life would make me too weak to deal with everything. My schoolwork continued to excel as I would go on to graduate with a GPA over 4.0, and teachers would constantly comment that I really took the time to understand what I was learning. I still had big dreams and big plans of what my life was going to be despite constantly being told and learning that kids who grow up in situations like mine don't get out.

Things never got easy, but they did get better throughout the rest of my high school experience. My mother's health started to stabilize by the end of high school, and she was able to pick up her own medication and cook for herself. She could survive without me. So I prepared for college.

After spending my freshman year of college in a small city, I decided to transfer to a university closer to home to better position myself for my future aspirations. It was a beautiful sunny day when the semester ended and I packed up my car to drive home. I had spoken previously with my mom about returning and staying with her, but I didn't anticipate how hazy her memory was because of her medication. When I pulled up and strolled into my mother's house, she forgot that I was moving back in. She had too many roommates already living with her—there were no open rooms in her house.

I felt hollow. The situation seemed like a cruel joke: I gave up three years of my life to care for her and here she was telling me, in a dazed state, that she didn't know I was coming back. Those three years did not earn a room in her home.

I ended up homeless at nineteen with what seemed like nowhere to go. I didn't feel like I could ask anyone for help. I couldn't bear the thought of looking at any family member in the eye. I felt like *I* was the failure. This wasn't supposed to happen to me; I had done everything right. I cried driving up the street, away from her home to I didn't know where.

At that moment, my identity cracked into more pieces than I ever thought could be repaired. I had no sense of direction, on the road or in my life. The locks that always existed around my mouth started to form around my heart. I was trapped again behind a door looking out the keyhole. I couldn't talk to anyone in my family—I felt too empty. Everything I had been told by those who doubted me and my future began to feel real. I wasn't going to get out of this storm. I'd worked endlessly to make my situations in life better: I was the 4.0 student; I was the athlete who lived for competition; I was the strong Christian who led his church groups in prayer; I was the caring son who gave up countless high school experiences to care for my mother; I was the child with dreams bigger than himself. But none of it mattered anymore.

Being 'homeless' lasted somewhere around one month, with me asking friends to use a couch or at least their floor. I would never tell the truth as to why I was asking to stay over to them or their parents, I would just say something along the lines of "I just don't want to go home." When I found some courage, I was able to find steadier housing between my father and my grandparents.

My enthusiasm for my plans in life waned after being homeless at nineteen. I struggled to find work despite my educational accomplishments throughout high school. Eventually, I was able to pick up work making pizza throughout college to ensure that I would never find myself without a place to sleep again. My life started to feel as circular as the pizzas I was making. My average week consisted of 35-40 hours of work wherein I would work shifts on Wednesday-Sunday that normally lasted from 4:00 PM to close (Which ranged anywhere from 11:30-1:00 AM depending on how fast we could finish cleaning up.) I would normally work a 3-hour shift on Monday with Tuesdays being my only day off. In addition to this, I was taking anywhere between 18-21 hours of classes. Since I was a transfer and changing majors, I had to play catch up to graduate in four years. This extreme schedule reduced my social life to null, and as I was working every night I made an agreement with myself that if I couldn't do homework while laying down, I wasn't going to do it.

My sophomore year of college was the worst performance in school that I had ever put in as I still managed a GPA over 3.0. But I could feel myself really struggling and not fully engaging in the work I was doing. Once I felt like I had a bit more financial backing I had asked to reduce my hours to 30 hours a week and by the start of my junior year I had capped my class schedule to only 18 hours a semester.

My grades would go on to improve as I graduated cum-laude from UNM's Anderson School of Business, and while I continued interviewing for internships, I couldn't find a start because of my lack of professional experience. The interviews never felt comfortable for me, either due to a lack of sleep or being fearful of my stutter coming out. The recruiters never seemed particularly interested in me and were unimpressed by my grades through college despite the improvement I showed in the business school while still maintaining a heavy work schedule. It seemed I lacked the pizazz they wanted in an employee. For the first time in my life, I wanted to quit. I was a failure at twenty before I even got my chance. My storm was bigger than my dreams.

When I was homeless, I spent one night sleeping in my car in front of a grocery store. I had no idea then that my balloon was on the horizon. I had no idea that in less than two years I would be advising at a corporate level, telling others how to run parts of their grocery business.

After finally hitting what felt like my lowest point, I got a phone call following a string of interviews from about a month before. The initial interview felt different than the others. The recruiter didn't want to discuss the generic topics that most interviews are filled with (What is your biggest strength? What is your biggest weakness? How have you reacted in X situation before? Etc...) Instead, he asked me to share a part of my life that reveals my character. With this stranger—who I had just met one day earlier at a recruiting event—I started talking about taking care of my mom in high school. My words never faltered, and sharing my story felt as natural as drinking water out of a glass. (It probably helped that the recruiter had the same first name as my father, Curt). I was invited to a second interview, where I was asked to share my story once again. After not hearing anything for a month, I assumed that I'd shared too much personal information. But when he called me back, he offered me an internship offer with a Fortune 500 Company, General Mills. After an hour-long conversation with a recruiter, he closed his pitch by telling me something along the lines of:

"I think you have a lot of potential, I feel you'll like the fit of the company for you. I'd like to extend an internship offer for you to come work with us over the summer in Arizona!"

I did it...

The words coming out of my mouth didn't sink me in my biggest moment. I accepted instantly and after exchanging a few more pleasantries we ended the call. I dropped to my knees and cried for an hour. Everything that I worked for and everything that I had strived for was coming to fruition. I had my chance.

My storm had run its course, the skies outside seemed to become clear after the call. It was the first time since I was homeless that I felt like my door had opened back up. I was no longer looking behind a keyhole, the door was open to the world outside. I started working on a couple other things in my life. I rebuilt the relationship I had with my mother, letting go of the anger I was holding on to— we were even able to live together for a short period of time during the remainder of my college career when she changed roommates. I started to spend more time with friends, no longer obsessing over but enjoying school. I started writing this book. After a summer of living my dreams in Arizona interning with General Mills, I received an official job offer.

That vision in the bright red balloon by little me has become my life.

The Balloon in the Storm

The Balloon in the Storm is about having vision for your life
And letting that guide you through your trials.
This book you are holding in your hands is my life.
The stories in between are based on the love I've felt.
The heartbreaks I've endured.
The triumphs I have earned by never giving up.
And the lessons they all have taught me.

If a poor mute boy can achieve his dreams, so can YOU!
I want you to know that your storm will end.
Even when it seems like it will never stop raining.
There is always a balloon in the storm.
You have to be willing to look for it though.

The stories you are about to read are based on the concepts
of what I shared above and more.
You will read stories about being born mute.
You will read stories about being born poor.
I hope these stories make you laugh.
I hope these stories make you cry (But only for like five seconds!)
And I hope, more than anything else,
that they make you believe in yourself.

BOOK I - THE BALLOON

THE BALLOON

The encompassing cool that the early morning brought begins to fade away. I let go of the onyx fleece blanket wrapping me up, and it falls into the truck bed. I'll grab it later, when the chase crew picks us up after the flight. I slide out of the back of the truck. I can still hear the bass from the front seat. The driver looks up, though I'm not sure if it was because of me. I walk closer to the burner. The steel pipes seem too modern on the woven basket. The warmth of the fire from the burner engine begins to fill the bottom opening of the beautiful fabric, stretched out across the morning grass. The woven red nylon blends like a knitter's morning dreams.

My breathing turns into little clouds, and I recall the thrill of childhood. I remember waiting at a bus stop, cracking jokes with my friends like there's no tomorrow. I remember the little clouds we'd form. I miss laughing like that. The pilot shouts to the rest of his crew as they remain anchored to the ropes stopping the balloon from take-off. A collective grunt breaks among them, as their muscles tighten pulling against the weight of the ropes. The balloon begins to rise, almost as if it's alive. I walk closer to the basket; the pilot calls me in. I can feel the other soon-to-be passengers stare at me, their eyes like a small fire burning my back as I step closer.

"Help me get the basket upright," the pilot says, as a trickle of sweat breaks against his forehead. He grabs a handkerchief from his back pocket and wipes. I grab the other end of the basket as we both push it upright onto the ground. I wipe my arm against my forehead after we get the basket up to make it seem like I spent more energy than I did. I didn't want him to think that it was easier for me than him. I take another deep breath with my head looking to the heavens. I remember I liked to pretend that the moisture from laughter around the world would add up, and on the cold days when it rained, each raindrop held a tinge of that happiness in it.

"Come on in," the pilot waves me and the rest of the passengers in with one light flick of his wrist. I struggle as I get into the basket, unsure of how my legs are supposed to cross over the edge. The other passengers look at me like I'm from a foreign place as I teeter over the basket's edge. I smile back, but they look down as they enter the basket.

Some of the crew move closer to grab the ends of the basket. The ground beneath me feels lighter with each crew member releasing their rope until all that's holding us down are hands.

Today the skies are clear as we brace for takeoff. I want to create some future clouds.

"There's nowhere to go from here but up," I say, wanting just one laugh.

The other passengers finally accept me as one of their own, a collective snicker ripples through the basket. We begin to soar through the sky.

A BOY AND HIS CAPE

It bounces like a red sea as Jax run circles in his 4x4 lawn, the only spot he is allowed to play in the backyard. It rises off his back as if that little red cape also believes it can help him fly. His room is filled with a boundless supply of model planes and spaceships, much to his mother's dismay as she holds hopes of a child's room she can walk into without fear of stepping on his dreams.

"My love," his mother calls, "I'll be back in an hour. Please stay close." Jax stares at her without a trace of promise in his eyes. He returns to his little game as his mother returns inside. A mischievous thought whips like wind against his mind as he stares at the forest hiding its treasures past his backyard. A cool chill invites him to come closer and experience the pleasure of crunchy brown leaves snapping against his shoes that await him just past the property line. Jax turns his head around as the promise of secrecy is granted by the car's ignition starting in the front of the house. He waits as he hears the sound of rubber and pavement taking his mother away. Jax takes a measured step outside of his 4x4 lawn as if the area outside of it were a landmine. After the first step though he gains a bit more courage and takes one more step forward, and another until he breaks out into a sprint toward the green treasure, with his red cape following close behind.

Snap, snap, snap. He is free! He raises his head to stare up as the trees begin to arch over him. It reminds him of a kaleidoscope as the branches allow slivers of light to break through in parts upon the forest's foliage. For the first time in his life he fully grasps the feeling his mother feels whenever she calls him "love" as he melts into the world around him. Jax sprints his way into a clearing where there are no trees blocking the sky, but residual leaves dragged there by the wind. Jax leaps with his red cape keeping him afloat into a pile of leaves, performing a human barrel roll as the leaves scatter around him. He wraps himself up with his red cape and stares up at the sky, his back against the crisp mixture of grass and leaves. The clouds float above him, and he opens his mouth with what should be a laugh that comes out, though he remains silent.

A troubling breeze causes Jax to shiver as he hears voices that are growing closer. He lifts his body up and searches for the faces that are bringing the sound. A group of four boys. He notes in his mind that all but one of them are a bit bigger than himself. They approach from within the same spot of the forest through which he entered the clearing. Jax places his arms over knees as he watches them grow closer. The leader of the pack notices Jax, and points at him saying something to the rest of his boys. They hasten their pace in his direction.

"Hey, I'm Mikey." Mikey places his hand out in front of him expecting Jax to return the shake as he looks back at the rest of the group to add, "And this is the Wolf Pack." The smallest of the Wolf Pack takes in a big sniff of snot before spitting it out behind him. Jax offers an empty stare with one eyebrow arched at Mikey's hand; his mouth opens, but no words leap off his tongue. After a few seconds, Jax closes his mouth and wraps the cape around his body, hiding all but his head, which pop out at the top.

"What's the matter with ya?" Mikey pulls back his hand and instead wraps it around his other arm in front of his chest. "Your daddy not teach you how to shake like a man?" Jax stares down at the ground and opens his mouth again with the hope that something will come out. An infantile grumble makes its way out of Jax, and an uncertain smile breaks across his face as he looks back up to Mikey and the Wolf Pack, hoping that it was enough for them.

"Seems like we got a little weirdo here, boys," Mikey announces while turning his back to Jax to face the Wolf Pack. A shared smile breaks across the faces of the other three boys as Mikey begins to rub his hands together like they're holding a plan. Mikey turns back to Jax, lunging at him with both arms outstretched, and pushes Jax to the ground. Jax's red cape picks up traces of the shrubbery around him, and he furrows his brow and stares at Mikey with a detached fire as he tightens his fist.

"What are you gonna do weirdo? Fight me!"

The Wolf Pack breaks into a shared laugh that dances around Jax's eardrums. Jax leaps from off the ground with his fist loaded, and aiming straight for Mikey's chin. His red cape lifts him again to deliver the blow, and knuckles meet chin like the bending of metal in a car crash. Mikey falls onto his butt with his eyes wide open. The shock of the punch leaves him looking paralyzed as if Jax's fists held venom. Jax, on the other hand, lands like a graceful airplane onto one knee, his red cape landing soft against his back. The Wolf Pack stares upon their almighty leader with anticipation, searching for what to do next.

"Get him, you idiots!" Mikey cries as he soothes his chin with the touch of his palm. Jax breaks back into a sprint past the Wolf Pack with them following suit into the forest. The red cape flows around him like a forcefield keeping the Wolf Pack at enough of a distance as leaves snap underneath their feet. The Wolf Pack howls behind him with hopes that their sound will propel them to run down Jax.

"Stop!" Mikey screams to the rest of the Wolf Pack. Jax looks behind his shoulder, still sprinting until he notices the ghostlike terror on the faces of the Wolf Pack. They begin backtracking and sprinting into the other direction, allowing Jax a few seconds to stop and catch his breath. A quiet growl causes the small hairs on his arms to stand at attention, each a small man of service. Jax attempts to let out a whimper, though silence is all that comes out as he looks upon the fulvous coat of a coyote.

The coyote begins to circle around Jax, who is quivering like a boat in water. Boy and beast closely eye each other. Jax attempts to scare off the coyote by shouting, but, again, when he opens his mouth silence fills the distance between the two. The coyote grimaces with a sense of deranged joy as he licks upon the fangs he brandishes at Jax. Jax's facial features grow tighter against his face as he stares, ready for the coyote, his arms now down at his sides. He begins to stomp his feet and then pulls his cape across himself like a matador awaiting his opponent. Finally, the coyote leaps toward Jax. Jax spins around and out of the way, much to the coyote's surprise. As the coyote misses on its initial leap, it finds Jax's tiny foot buried deep into its chest.

Jax sprints in the opposite direction towards home. Tears stream across both sides of his face as he makes his way out of the forest. The world goes mute. All that exists is the tension in Jax's legs as he sees the clearing from which he entered the day. As he escapes from the tree arches into his backyard, sounds begin to pour back into his life like colors to his ears. There is no sound of leaves snapping behind him, though that doesn't stop his sprint as he makes his way to the back door. Jax reaches up and shakes the door handle though it doesn't budge—it's locked. He takes a deep breath and turns around to stare out at the forest. His eyes are two large disks as he presses his back against his home, sneaking around with timed steps to the front of the house. His breaths become easier when he passes around the corner and sees his mother's car sitting quiet in its lot. Jax peels his back off the house and enters a normal walking pace toward the front door.

The deck light flickers, and Jax sees his mother resting with her elbows against the cap rail. Her eyes whisper that they are tired as a light smile stretches across her face. Jax's eyes begin watering as he runs up the stairs to the top of the deck. His cape flies off from around his neck and falters to the bottom of the steps. He stares at his mother, wanting to share everything. A few tears glide across his chin with his mouth agape, like a boulder surrounded by a rushing white river.

"My love," his mother says, "with those who love you, every word, even unspoken, is still understood." Her arms surround him. He is whole.

KINTSUGI (CRACKS)

A bronze wolf statue stares over the pond, alone atop its quiet green hill. The wolf is frozen with its chest pushed out like a leader prepared for battle. An older gentleman wearing a brown fedora looks up at the wolf from the end of a bridge that lays across the pond, taking a break from cracking the bread in his hand to feed a family of ducks. A delicate quack presses like hands against his ears. His eyes trail away toward a baby duck batting its wings, too small to fly just yet. The baby duck continues to try but can't get much separation from the ground. The man smiles as he bends closer to the baby duck. Its tiny legs waddle closer to him. He could swear the duck's bill forms a smile as he brushes the fuzzy yellow head.

"Aren't you a cute little guy," the man says, offering some crumbs to the baby duck. His face turns into a puzzled joy. The baby duck stares at him with the crumbs in his mouth, not daring to chew down on them. Again, the baby duck appears to be a bit human as it seems to nod at the man. The older gentleman lets out a laugh under his breath, left in disbelief as the baby duck waddles off, still not having eaten the crumbs. The baby duck turns left behind a concrete seating area. The man makes his way across the bridge, ready to go home as he's received his share of smiles for the day.

The baby duck fumbles over its unseasoned feet as it approaches a larger duck that is hiding behind the concrete wall. A collection of fallen feathers surround the resting body of the mother duck. The baby duck gathers its footing as a nasty cough escapes from the mother duck. The duckling looks up to its mother wishing it could heal her illness. The food is dropped in front of the mother duck's face, and the baby duck nuzzles closer to the body of its mother, it shivers as her body provides no warmth. Night approaches from the east as the baby duck's eyes droop like leaves in the summer. A warm wind slides in, blowing the duckling's eyes to sleep.

A growl like a rusted lawn mower starting up breaks the silence of midnight. The baby duck's eyes jumble as though they were shaken in a bingo blower. The sound is coming from his mother, her eyes puncturing the nighttime black as a ruby in the sky, her feathers swooshing as she flashes them out, making herself big. The brown and white arrow design of her feathers shine with the moon against the gray concrete. The duckling's eyes stop moving as it senses a warning, forcing it to look up at its mother. The beak of its mother jabs down at the baby duck's neck. The duckling rolls backwards landing on its stomach to avoid the midnight assault. A quack as soft as skin rolls out of the baby duck as its stomach hits the ground. The mother quacks in response but her quacks sound like a broken chew toy.

The mother moves slow as she realigns her ruby eyes to the baby ducks neck like a laser. The baby duck fixes its footing and sprints a couple paces away. It remains still for a few moments, before pointing with his wing at her, shaking with anger as he pleads for an answer. A quack breaks loose from its throat to break the tension of silence. The duckling's mother begins to sound more like a dog as the growl returns and she braces her legs. The baby duck sprints out towards the hill before his mother can react, and his mother follows suit though her body cannot respond as she wishes. The mother's growl turns into a wheeze as her lungs feel like they're collapsing while the baby duck continues to gain distance as it makes its way up the hill.—first ten feet, then twenty, then thirty feet between them. Finally, his mother returns back to the concrete wall. A flurry of discolored feathers popping up around her as she flops herself back down to sleep.

The baby duck finds its way to the top. Staring in a mix of fear and awe, as if the emotions were blending together in a big black pot, at the bronze wolf. The baby duck waddles underneath the statue. The duckling cocks its head to the side as it notices the area underneath the wolf's belly felt warm like a fleece blanket on a winter night. The baby duck begins chirping in a series of three, gentle like honey for the ear, its tiny tail wagging up and down to each chirp, and its eyes melting to shapes like almonds. The baby duck lays itself down underneath the center of the belly, drifting away to a better dream.

As the sun replaces the moon from the east. The water from the pond glimmers its warm greeting, "Good morning." The duckling's mother is gone, and only a tuft of feathers where she rested is visible. The baby duck rises and waddles out from underneath the statue, delicate with each step to not wake any other creatures this morning.

The baby duck walks to the back of the wolf. It pauses for a moment and then breaks into a sprint aimed at the hind legs of the statue. The baby duck makes its way up onto the back of the wolf and stares out over the pond. The duckling believes mother is hiding, lamenting as she wishes she had told her offspring to be safe. The baby duck dreams of the gentle yet warm morning wind telling him "Join me." He takes one last look over the pond with the orange rays of sunlight bouncing off like the flash of a camera.

The baby duck sprints off the edge and bursts into flight. He doesn't need to go home.

———

Nothing will ever crack my heart the same way as caring for my mom on her proposed (though, thankfully, false) deathbed as a teenager, only to return later and be told that she does not have room for me in her home.

Finding my own path in life and learning to forgive her filled my cracks with gold.

MY WORDS ARE LIKE APPLE CHUTNEY

"Have I ever told you why I'm so fascinated with music and singing?" My eyes fixate on the apple as it learns of the gravity between my hand and the air above it. I stop the toss to look towards Oliver, who is filling his silver backpack on his bunk.

"Hmmm, I'm not sure you have Alan," Oliver replies, his eyes stop on the vivacious red of the apple before turning towards my direction. The red draws us both in. He should be running along to his next class but I've piqued his interest. "What about it fascinates you?" He returns to loading his pack.

I lean forward on the aged wooden chair that we ransacked from the cafeteria—the school would never notice. I place the apple in both hands and between my knees. A storm begins to brew as I take in a breath, fearing the stutter that could collapse me.

"Everything," I say, and it feels like a piece of ice leaving my mouth and entering his ear. He stops packing and turns with a slight raise of his left eyebrow upon his face. I lost control of my voice's tone and the word sounds too cold.

"Real descriptive their bud, aren't ya?" he sneers, knowing I struggle with my words.

"Everything," I repeat "Everything about the voice," a chill continues to circle the rooms as Oliver shivers.

"Hmm. Care to elaborate," his features turn softer as the sneer is replaced by a smile that embraces me like we hadn't seen each other in years.

"Everything they say is prepared," my words start to sound a bit warmer, "They can say exactly what they mean after perhaps years of writing and re-writing the same line dozens of times." I shake the apple in rhythm with the words coming out of my mouth, as if the red of the apple were shaping my mouth in ways that I'm not able to. "And then after, the words have felt the eternal love that exists between pen and paper. A secret kept yet somehow shared between them." My body shakes as if the words I'm saying are opening that secret for the first time. "But then after the words are set, you prepare and prepare, finding exactly where the letters need to be, maybe a little high and maybe a little low."

"Your thoughts are interesting." Oliver says still sporting his smile, and I know that he understands. He rustles his long brown hair with his left hand.

"It gives me the time I need to prepare the muscles in my mouth to mask this stutter." I look down upon the apple, in fear that it will stop sharing its energy as I feel it guiding me through the conversation. "I don't have to fret over the nervousness that wrinkles itself in my normal voice. It captures my beliefs as confidently as they are in my head, unlike when I speak."

Oliver returns to his packing after he looks at his watch, realizing he's going to be running into a classroom that's already begun its bustle of the day.

"You worry a bit too much about it."

I lean back into the chair and begin to wonder again along with the apple about the battles of gravity.

"I bi... I bi... I mean" I pause for a moment "I have big dreams" I take a bite of the apple and toss it over to Oliver. A smile erupts on my face like there is still a bit of that secret I didn't share.

THE MOUNTAIN

A brief shiver rolls down off of her shoulders to the heels of her feet as she trudges on through the mountain cold. Her name is Ava—the peaks of each letters as sharp as her drive. Her breaths form little clouds she wishes she could reclaim for warmth. But the mountain steals them.

Her journey is lasting longer than she anticipated, but the only thing that matters to her is getting to the top of the mountain. Her feet ache as they continue to beat onto the ground like a car with a pierced tire on asphalt. Her pace lessens as her lungs feel too strained from the frigid air that wraps its claws around her throat. The claws retract as she bends over; her breath feels warmer as she clutches her knees. Her entire body trembles—even the smallest of hairs laying against the back of her neck shift a bit as she pushes herself up. Short staggered steps guide her to an ice-covered rock to lean against for a moment of recharge. She grimaces behind her face shield; the skull decal on the face shield maintains a smile though. The pain from the cold cuts into her bones like a million sharpened knifes drilling their way past her coats. Despite the pain she feels pressed against her, she doesn't hesitate to take in the view before her.

The sun hangs low as it approaches from the east. It taunts her with those false flames, not coming close enough to her this high up. The white ground plays a deafened drone as the sun pretends to melt it. Ava's eyes adjust to the oncoming brightness that reveals how high up she has made it so far. She notices the magic of snow packed tight and untouched, a deep stillness filling her as the silence rings from one end of her head to the other. The silence unnerves her as it makes her inner voice sound so loud. She laughs to break the delicate line of quiet, and it calms her thoughts. The sound of laughter loops around her after it bounces off the snow and makes her feel dizzy. She wonders why others don't try to get up this high and feel the earth like this.

This is it. All of the hard work and dedication that she has put in—it is bound to pay off in an ever-approaching moment. Ava is certain that the top of the mountain is up past the next bend. Her eyes begin to water, leaving a trail of steam circling around her head. Her body is going numb, perhaps from the cold or maybe the surge of her emotions—feelings that have been pushed so far down for the past year that she felt shut off from the rest of the world. For the past year, her light bulb for everything else about life flicked off. All that remained of her was an obsession: her obsession to prove she is more than others think. For her entire life, everyone doubted her. Petite and timid Ava could never be as strong or brave as her younger sister, Kodi. She needed to prove to Kodi that she could do this. She needed to climb this mountain more than she needed to breathe.

"Av... Are you awake?" Kodi's fingers prodding against her face forces Ava to wake up. Ava flips her pillow over, whacking

Kodi in the face as she switches sides. Kodi studies the sluggish Ava for a moment as if her sister is an animal about to be hunted. Kodi grabs both ends of the cover at the bottom of the bed and leaps to the front of the bed, swallowing up Ava with the sheets.

Ava wrestles underneath the sheets to no avail. Her face flashing red as she grows angrier. She punches from beneath the sheet, though she can't land a single one on her sister. "Kodi! Let me out!" Ava screamed. The sheets finally open as Kodi falls off, erupting with laughter at her sister's ineptitude.

"You promised to go explore with me today!" Kodi smiles at Ava as if she wasn't just torturing her seconds ago. She slides off the bed and makes her way over to Ava's dresser. The look of confusion takes hold of her face as she combs through Ava's make-up collection. "You're such a princess." Kodi mocks with a high-pitched voice as she picks up a mirror from Ava's dresser.

Ava tucks her arms behind her knees as she sits up on her bed and stares at her younger sister. Despite being five years her junior, Kodi is taller than her with muscles bigger than most of the boys in Kodi's 6th grade classes. "Oh yeah? Well aren't you quite the prince charming."

Kodi's head drops as if she's become a ragdoll when Ava speaks those words. Kodi always drifted around a fine line of sensitivity by being able to compete with the boys while never wanting to be considered one of them. The mirror in her hands drops and smashes against the floor with pieces scattering across the room, Ava's sneer hit a tender spot in Kodi's chest. She remains silent as a few tears hit the floor.

Ava jumps out of bed and runs to her sister, stepping with care to avoid the glass. "Oh Kodi... You know you're a princess." Ava wipes away the tears and held her sister's face in her hands. "And such a pretty one too."

Kodi breaks away from Ava's grasp. "Whatever... Just get ready so we can go." Kodi makes her way to Ava's doorway and grins back. "Can you try to actually keep up with me today though?"

Ava smiles as she starts to get ready. She secretly enjoys how much Kodi pushes her.

A sinking feeling anchors down her mind as her vision clears from the steam. Her eyes flinch as she weighs the sacrifices of her work: the restless nights, the endless preparations, the lonesome training—not to mention the solitary confinement she built in her mind for the past year to keep herself focused on this goal. "This wasn't for nothing," she thinks, an uncomfortable chuckle escaping her mouth as though she is barely able to believe herself.

She tries to push her body away from the rock to continue her climb. Her legs won't move, almost as though they are glued to the ground. Her arms reach behind herself and push against the rock to no avail. She shrinks down onto her knees, bent at her core but unable to flex anything past her knees. Her breath is a drum kicking off a ritual, pounding faster and faster against the cold. She motions up as fast as she can to jump, but her body recoils and she ends up seated in the snow. She thrashes her fists into the snow at her sides, a flurry of snow kicking against her face shield. Each flake bites like a tiny white piranha against the fabric. She feels as trapped as the crystallized tear that sparkles near her eye duct. Her life starts to flash before her eyes.

"I want to climb a big, snowy mountain someday" Kodi keeps her eyes forward as she leads Ava into the forest behind their home. When she is outside, her legs move as naturally as a writer's fingers across a typewriter in a fit of creativity. It appears she never steps onto faulty branches or hidden crevices, like the forest speaks to her in a way that guides her safely through it.

"Oh yeah? Which one Kodi?" Ava asks while following behind.

"I don't know yet. But a big one! I want it to be a challenge." Kodi doesn't look away from the path in front of her, if she did she would notice Ava struggling to keep pace with her.

"You've always been such a risk-taker... I don't know if I could ever be brave enough to climb a mountain alone, especially not a big one," says Ava.

"You could. You just need to be brave for a few moments when you start to climb. Then you won't know how to stop. That's what I always tell myself at least." The sounds of the forest replace their conversation as they remain silent for the rest of their walk.

Kodi stops as she approaches the edge of a ravine. Tears fall from her face as she appreciates the blending of green and blue at the bottom of the ravine. "It's so peaceful here." Ava catches up and stares down into the depth of the ravine.

Ava slides down next to Kodi, "It really is... Can I ask you something?"

"What's up?"

"Whichever mountain you choose, can I climb it with you?" Ava waits for a response as Kodi turns to her sister for the first time since they started exploring today, and she smiles.

"Yes. Definitely." Kodi cradles herself into her sister's shoulder.

"We can train together for it." Ava brushes at her sister's hair, "This has been fun."

"Do you see that bridge over there? I've never seen that before. Let's go check it out!" Before Ava can respond her sister is already sprinting for the bridge.

Her breaths are heavy as she catches up to Kodi at the foot of the bridge, and when she sees the condition of it, her stomach turns. Some of the boards look warped and others are smashed along the edges. The ropes that hold the bridge together are a greenish-black as if they are molded. "Kodi we can't go on this bridge."

"You don't have too, but I'm going to." Kodi grabs at the ropes, trusting her instincts, and steps onto the first board. "I want to see what's on the other side of the ravine." The board creaks as if it's placing a spell on her. Each step she takes seem to cast more incantations calling her to continue.

Ava's hands shake as she watches her sister, "Kodi! Get back here! That's not safe!"

"I'm fine!" she continues forward, the creaks start to sound more like a chant.

"Kodi! I'm not joking! Get off that thing now!" Ava's cheeks feel strained as she watches in dread while her sister walks to the middle of the

The Balloon in the Storm

bridge. Kodi stops to face her sister. The creaks of the bridge do not stop though; they only grow louder. The sound turns into a snap as the board beneath her feet gives way. She falls through the bottom but grabs onto the closest board with her hands. She holds herself up with her arms. "Kodi! I'm coming to get you."

"Ava!" Kodi's eyes fill with tears as she holds on with all her might.

Ava grabs at the ropes, but it is too late. Time seems to slow down as the board Kodi is holding onto cracks, the sound like a single gunshot in Ava's ears as she watches her sister float down to the bottom of the ravine. Ava's vision becomes like a crystal ball as she looks out at her sister for the last time, with a blue mist filling up and pouring out of the glass.

A snowstorm begins to dare of its entrance, and she worries that she is going to die here, alone. The fire inside her head burns low as she looks for the matches in her mind, hoping to relight the flame. She knows she misplaced them behind less important thoughts. "I could just lay here," she thinks, but an image quickly flashes in front of her: her face shield aligned perfectly with her own skull, her lifeless bones, the horror on the face of the stranger who discovers her. She would become known as the woman who failed to climb the mountain.

Visions of a face she could never forget begin to surface, and she looks into Kodi's untroubled olive-colored eyes. They make her feel like she is sitting in front of a fireplace with their mother about to call them both into the kitchen for a cup of cocoa. Ava notices the tightness in her lungs and wonders if she might be running out of oxygen soon. Each breath feels heavy, as the oxygen races down the mountainside away from her. To distract herself, she inspects the rest of Kodi's face. She misses Kodi's round cheeks and her tiny button-like nose. She lets out a light moan of pain as the image whistles away with a wisp of chilled wind.

The connection with her sister reveals where she left one of those matches, and a light spark begins to fizzle between her head. Still her body can't garner the energy to sit up, but she feels like she will be able to soon. Her heart believes that Kodi's spirit is still with her and will give her the strength to finish this. A sense of Zen starts to melt at the snow around her bottom.

"I quit. I'm done dealing with you." Ava's cousin, Brett, unfastens the gloves on his hands. He throws them down onto the mat Ava is sitting down on. "It feels like you aren't even trying anymore."

"I am trying, Brett." her words are harsh as she lays back against the mat. "I'm just sore today."

"You've had four days off! You can't be that sore."

"Well, I am."

"It's been four months since you first asked me for help and you still can't even finish a single climb in my gym." Brett smacks the back of one hand into the other's palm. Ava leans back up but doesn't know what to respond. "Look, I've wanted to help you since we all lost Kodi. But at this point, I feel like this is just going to be another thing you quit."

Ava's eyes start to water "That's not true."

"You quit when you played soccer. You quit when you were trying to learn the violin. You quit after you asked my dad to teach you how to cook. I mean, Ava you barely even graduated high school."

"We had just lost Kodi..."

"I'm sorry Ava, you know I know better than anyone else. You do realize I lost my best friend after Kodi's fall too right? She was the only one in the family who would come climb with me. I stopped climbing for a year after she passed."

"I get it Brent."

"Do you? It took me a lot to start climbing again. But now look, it's been five years and I opened my own climbing gym in her honor. Because I know she would have wanted me to do something with that hurt."

"Okay, Brent."

"Look Ava we all have been struggling for years but you have to try if you want this. More than anything else." Brent feels his words trailing off as he thinks about Kodi.

"I didn't even care about any of those things!" Ava defends.

"Somehow, this doesn't feel any different." Brett turns and walk away, leaving Ava alone on the mat. She wipes away the few tears that crept out. She gets up and walks over to the rock wall.

"I can do this," Ava whispers to herself "For Kodi." For the first time in her life she feels a fire burning inside of her. She presses herself against the wall and it feels like she has Kodi's muscles. Each rock up, though a challenge, does not deter her to stop. Ava doesn't even realize that she is passing her highest point with ease. She sees the bell at the top of the climb is only two rocks away. She scales the rocks without hesitation and, before she knows it, she is ringing the bell. She has never felt more alive. The rings are a joyous melody as she dismounts and descends to the mat below.

"I'm proud of you," Brett says. He reappeared while Ava was climbing. "I want to keep helping you. But I need you to keep trying like that."

"I will. I have too. For Kodi." Ava nods her head but doesn't look up from the mat.

"Ayyye can you hear me? Hello!" a familiar voice rings like a phone off the hook, "Is there anybody home in there?" The pressure of a finger about to press against her forehead shot open Ava's eyes. An adult version of Kodi peers from above, just inches away from Ava's face. "So are you alright? I assume you're gonna get up soon since the floor must be freezing!" she says, giggling to herself as she holds the false belief that she's said something clever. The outstretched hand on her shoulder from Kodi feels so warm—the match. Kodi remains giggling as Ava removes her back from the snow by pushing against the ground with her elbows. She grabs around each knee with both of her hands and plucks one leg at a time out of the ground, the same way a botanist would pull out flowers in May. Kodi's laugh reminds Ava of a time when everything was for the sake of play. Ava feels as if she's been hit by a flash bang while in her presence. The mountain ground spins beneath her as the silent drone of the mountain snow begins to get louder. Kodi grabs Ava's arm and lifts her up the rest of the mountain. They aren't far away. "Can't believe you almost gave up at the top," Kodi beams like a mischievous cat. Ava would cry if the winter cold would stop freezing the water. "It's okay! You got this far on your own. I want to help you finish." Ava looks down and the tears break through the shackles of the cold. And just like that, Kodi is gone again.

Their short-lived trek together to the top brings Ava less than a foot away from the edge, and an empty abyss of dark mist is all that lays below. She did it. Once her eyes and brain connect how close she is to the edge, she jumps out of her own skin as her body drops to the ground. She punches both of her hands into the snow behind like anchors. She drags herself one hand at a time backwards, away from the edge. Her entire body buzzes like the vibration of gold being rolled against her skin. She wants to sleep, but first she wants to tell the world that she made it.

"Hey!" an unknown man with flight gear approaches her, "We've been waiting on you!" Ava's lungs feel too tight to respond; her breaths are staggered as the oxygen continues to run away from her body and down the bottom of the mountain. "Congratulations on your finish! We started to get worried. We were expecting you hours ago." The man wraps a fleece blanket around her and scoops her up. They walk to the opposite end of the mountaintop to the tune of chopped air. An additional pilot stares down at them from the cockpit of the helicopter. The man doesn't struggle at all as he steps up into the back of the helicopter with her wrapped up body in his arms. He feels warm against her frozen coats. The man grabs an oxygen mask and moves her face shield down. He places the oxygen over her head to give her more life. She takes a deep breath to soak up the oxygen that couldn't escape her now. Her eyes motion him over, and he leans in closer.

"I can't believe I really did it," she whispers with what she can muster "Kodi helped me." The man smiles with a light crispness at the corners of his lips. He signals at the pilot up front to continue forward.

THE ROOM THAT SPINS SONGS

A camp guide leads my class deeper into the woods. I marvel at the beauty of the trees and daydream about climbing them instead of listening to the guide as talks about the room he's leading us to for choir practice. He looks excited as he tells us all about its "magic." I can hardly pay attention as he continues. How could a tiny room hold more magic than this whole forest out here? If it were up to me, I'd have us all just stay outside to sing. We finally arrive, and the guide opens the door.

It is an empty room with the chair and cupboard being the only consistent inhabitants. There's more dust in here than there are leaves in this entire forest. I sigh as it feels like the guide built up too much excitement for this. I'm surprised our teacher took us out on a field trip to come sing in this room. Our normal classroom is great compared to this. There's no magic hidden here. I want to go back outside.

Our instructor, Ms. Ferris, gathers us all around her in a circle. She tells us to not just sing, but to breathe life into the song we are about to sing. I look around once more at the tiny room.

Ms. Ferris starts counting off "1...2...3..." the combination of us all—Karla, Shae, Marley, Abel, Nick, and I begin to sing our modern rendition of "Shine on Harvest Moon."

The Balloon in the Storm

The night was mighty dark so you could hardly see

Ms. Ferris looks directly into one of the girl's eyes and moves her hands as if she is conducting an entire symphony instead of an odd collection of high-schoolers.

For the moon refused to shine.

Her feet trace along the wooden floor like a tiny dancer. Ms. Ferris begins to move in a circular formation and, one at a time, we all manage to lock eyes with her.

Couple sitting underneath a willow tree

Hours and hours of practice in our classroom culminated into this oaky moment.

For love they did pine.

Everyone's focus intensifies as Ms. Ferris grabs at our souls, a grim reaper of sorts. Her eyes pulling us deeper into the room, into the song. She pays careful attention to each one of us, staring one by one. She spins her hands as it corrects each person's tune to a perfect synchronization of timing and key.

Little maid was kinda 'fraid of darkness

Our voices reflect off the wooden interior of the room. The room feels as if it is starting to spin, our voices the wheels moving it around and around.

So she said, "I guess I'll go."

Shae had always been able to sing the highest. Her voice bounces around the room creating a prism. Rainbows of sound flowing into our ears.

Boy began to sigh, looked up at the sky,

A bird from the outside forest of the campsite begins to join in our song with an ambient chirping.

And told the moon his little tale of woe

Karla begins to tear up as we near the chorus of the song. The tears burst through as we hit the first note of the chorus like a dam that's lost its battle.

Oh, Shine on, shine on, harvest moon
Up in the sky;
I ain't had no lovin'
Since April, January, June or July.

It's only midday and the sun is peering through the giant glass window that takes up the majority of one of the walls. I notice the brown oak floors as the sunlight makes it look radiant. Ms. Ferris tells us all to close our eyes as we jump into the end of the chorus.

Snow time, ain't no time to stay

Not a single voice is cracking or faltering. The air feels heavy.

Outdoors and spoon;

The rustle of outside leaves does not dare to break through to the room as fellow students walk along the perimeter of the cabin.

So shine on, shine on, harvest moon,.

Ms. Ferris steps aside from her guiding role to an old-fashioned wooden chair fixed near the window. No one stops singing. She breathes soft with slow tears taking in the moment. Her eyes still like a porcelain doll as she becomes lost in the music.

For me and my gal.

The second chorus erupts from tearful eyes.

Oh, Shine on, shine on, harvest moon
Up in the sky;
I ain't had no lovin'
Since April, January, June or July.

An old cupboard stands in the back of the room. Various trinkets and knick-knacks loiter the shelves for everyone to see. The sensation of spinning begins to ease as the song nears its end. The room becomes more distinct through my eyes.

Snow time, ain't no time to stay

Outdoors and spoon;

The girls fade out on that last note. Abel, Nick, and I close out the song with our deeper male voices. The room halting to a stop.

So shine on, shine on, harvest moon,

For me and my gal.

The acoustic echo of our bass notes linger for a moment before everyone seems to break out of our group trance. Ms. Ferris, in her typical fashion, tears up again and congratulates us on one of our best performances we've ever shared as a group.

The room continues to buzz as everyone embraces each other. No one seems willing to leave the room, maybe we're all a little afraid to leave this moment. I can't believe that I wanted to sing outside. I would have missed the hidden beauty in the room that spins song.

TWENTY MINUTES

Is this even real... twenty more minutes... could that be all I have left... what a damper this puts into the rest of my day. Well actually, I guess the rest of my hour... On the bright side at least I no longer have to write up that report since it will all be over soon I guess. Though I'm conflicted... I did actually like that project. My manager said it was my best work yet.

The sun feels warms against my face from my office's rooftop patio. I stare out at a clock that is sitting in the middle of the sky. Everyone else has already fled from the office—they seem to believe that the clock is counting down the remainder of time we all have left. As I stare at the numbers, I feel a pit in my stomach that feels like it can never be filled. This isn't fair; I don't feel like I have had enough time. I return inside to break the anxiety I am starting to feel.

I pull the name tag off of my chest. 'Alex' it reads, and, I place it next to my keyboard. I stare at the 'Y' key for longer than what might be considered a normal amount to do such a thing, especially right now, when time is limited. I break my gaze, only to get lost in the buzz of blue computer screen light for a moment. I'm not sure how, but out of nowhere, an image of the same clock that's outside pops up on my screen—that round golden clock with grim black numbers counting down.

I tap the pop up away and click on the internet browser to see if the news has any updates.

According to the internet it'd be best to get out of the office since every online news source is now synced to the timing of the mystic clock terrorizing the sky. My eyes scrunch against the computer screen as I read an article on a website. The writer, like the rest of us, is unsure of where the clock came from. The article mentions that the clock's surface area appears the same size and distance away from all angles in every country it's had its picture taken. Eighteen o' one, eighteen, seventeen fifty-nine, oh god... I really need to do something more if this is really going to be the end of it all.

With a sigh like I haven't worked out in months (I haven't, not that it matters now), I get out of my chair and make my way to the staircase to get out of the accounting firm. As I pass my manager's cubicle, I hear a couple people still tapping at their keyboards. My manager's seat is empty. He left the screen unlocked with the clock still counting down. It feels like the clock watches over me as well as he did. I turn my head across from my manager's cube and see the back of his counterpart's head. She must have closed the window on the computer that the clock popped up in. She is one of the three remaining key tappers, their taps like a sad song with no beat or rhythm. I somehow move in unison with their song to the door of the stairwell.

I wind down the stairs like a yo-yo on a string. I don't want to leave—it was hard work to get this job. As I hit the last step and open the door, I pause to breathe in deeply again. (I really should have gone to the gym more. It's not like I'm fat, just a little shapely. A roundish shape, like a sturdy peanut. But again, what does it matter now?) It appears that many of my co-workers went into a frenzy with the imminent threat of death approaching all of us. The skid marks of tires line the parking lot. Two cars are smashed together, connected at the noses of the cars. The keys left in the ignition of one of the cars, it is clicking faster than the rhythm of the clock. Why anyone would spend any of their last twenty minutes crammed into a metal box with wheels is beyond my mental comprehension. Sixteen forty-two... sixteen forty-one... sixteen forty... it won't stop.

I know what I what to do. I notice the buzzing coming from my pocket. I click on the candy red 'End' button. I scroll down the list of contacts to G. I text my grandma, "I love you Nan. Give the family my love." I stare for a moment waiting for a sound like liquid in a tube to confirm that it sent. Schwoop! The phone begins to vibrate against my hand, angry with me that I didn't accept the last call. I chuck it into the road, and it spins for four rotations before it's smashed by a dark orange car. I hop over a concrete slab onto a patch of grass. I hope Nan understands why I didn't call. If I couldn't be in her company, I'd rather her enjoy the love of everyone else already with her. I can feel her hands clasped together from miles away, as she thinks of me at this very second. She must have got my text.

I guess I'm in luck with everyone else falling into the disarray of time. My favorite park is emptier than school on a Sunday. I've been coming here since I was a kid. I picture a little me zooming across the greens and yellows of the ground and sky. I loved making Nan smile. I was always her favorite little rocket ship. She used to take me here because her husband designed the park. He was gone before I arrived. The man had a brilliant mind, an architect of the world outside, the placement of the trees his greatest masterpiece. All the nearby streets and buildings of the city are made invisible in the left pocket of the park. In the deepest corner of that patch there is one tree I like to sit under that I swore the tree architect must have designed just for me. It's as if he knew that his grandson would enjoy the view. When I sit with my back against the trunk and my head cocked to the right I can see the mountains. The cool misty blue of these gargantuan creatures of land were one of the few things in life that made me smile, a genuine smile that radiates off an entire person as it screams of happiness like a firefly buzzing in a jar on the fourth of July. That's what I wanted, to feel like a firework. Burning out with one of the happiest memories I could ever imagine. I wish I could thank my Grandpa, for planting that seed. Twelve o' two... Twelve o' one... Twelve... I stare at the clock before getting lost in the trees.

I make my way into that closed green pocket and plop myself down in my spot. I settle myself into a comfortable position shrugging my shoulders. I begin to turn my head to the right as I feel the sensation of something peering over me. It feels like a pair of curious eyes are prying into me like their newest novel. A strange oversized black bird with sparkling gold eyes that look bigger than mine is sitting next to me. It looks upon me from a closer distance than any other bird has ever been. As my eyes study the black bird I feel that same pit in my stomach from when I first saw the clock. Each small movement the bird makes reminds me of a second's hand on a clock, calculated and in rhythm. I reach out, and to my surprise it doesn't fly away the instant my fingers fall upon its body. I pat over its feathers and it feels like I am coming to life for the first time. The experience makes my heart pound against my chest with no recognition from the bird towards my gesture; it just continues to look upon me. Its glare makes the pit in my stomach feel like it's digging deeper, so I finally withdraw my hand. With a sharp note the bird caws and I swear I understand what he is saying. It's like he is warning me that all of time is almost up.

I feel myself wanting to cry, but my eyes are dry. I close my eyes tightly to rid the sinking feeling. When I reopen them, the bird is gone. I scan the circumference of the tree, crawling on my knees as I search for the bird. I remember it being right by my side only a moment ago. I must be losing my mind with the ever-increasing realization that I'll be gone soon. I lean back against the tree. It feels smooth and welcoming as if it is the hand of my grandfather and not just tree bark. I feel less alone with the thought of him looking over me. The unease in my stomach dies down and I can breathe like normal. I cannot see the clock from within these trees. Maybe time will never end.

I close my eyes and lean against the trunk. I feel so free that I want to cry. Maybe I'm already dead and I didn't notice. It feels like I'm aging backwards as parts of me seems to float away. First my worries, then my remorse. I'm worried about the moment my desire for independence floats away too.

I hear the tussle of knees crawling against leaves. I open my eyes and see the crown of a woman's head. She slides in next to me and doesn't say a word while looking in the opposite direction of me. I can see my desire for independence float away, I imagine a letter at a time from the word 'independence' hitting all the branches on the way up.

"I don't want to talk," she says brushing her hair out of her eyes.

"You don't have to" I say, neither of us willing to look away from our unimportant spots.

"I don't want to die alone," she cries but I can only sense the tears. She mutes the cry. I wasn't going to judge her. She rests her head against my shoulder.

"I don't know you, but I want you to know... that I'm still going to miss you..." my eyes feel strained as I shift away from the unimportant spots. I don't even remember what I was staring at. I stare at her auburn hair for a couple seconds, before finding another unimportant spot. Her head feels heavy and full, yet soft and free against my arm.

"Please, just don't go away" she whispers it to me, though it sounds like her words are for someone, some*thing*, else.

Neither of us attempts to talk for the remainder of our time sitting there, but the warmth of the other's body makes us both feel clean in the end. It feels like we've both made a secret promise to a child, the kind you can't break. I think I might have that feeling I wanted, to be like a firework. But I think I only have it because I'm sharing this moment with someone else.

In unison our eyes shift toward the mountain and it feels like time lasts forever. I can't think of anything past the utter calm of misty blue mountains and friendship. I see the bird again though, flying across my eyes over the mountain. Its golden eyes yearn for another tree.

Three. Two. One...

I NEED A HAPPY SATURDAY
(PART I - ENFP)

A dog is barking in the background. Two women walk towards neon lights without a care in their eyes. The night is still young as the sun flickers off to another horizon like a candle burning to the end of a jar. "Red Lines Brewery" radiates bright like whiskey in a fire as the women walk under the sign and into the bar. Wrapped up in gray winter pea coats, they are both beautiful, but it's beyond just their physical appearances. Their energy is air, filling the most destitute of lungs with enough energy to run ten marathons in that moment. But one of them, Carol, has a smile that sobers a man up and then hits like another shot of whiskey left sitting right in the chest. Tonight, though, her smile hides the yearning she holds for something new. She can't quite put her finger on what it is she is missing, but she knows there is an adventure waiting for her.

Carol is the older of the two, and she can't hold her tongue as she shares the tides of her day. Her voice captivates Sherryl. She looks upon her friend enraptured by the illuminous narrative of Carol's awkward first interaction with her new manager, who Carol ran into with a cup full of warm coffee upon meeting. As Carol builds to the climax the server chimes in:

"What can I get you ladies?" He wears a ponytail that makes him seem lost, as if he is the reincarnate of some archaic 70's rock band that never quite made it big enough.

"What kind of B.A. stouts do you have?" Carol asks as she leans in closer to him against the counter, placing both of her index fingers together and then against her lips awaiting his response, her eyes shining as she awaits the options.

"We got one right now—it's an Imperial Stout." His eyes shift to a co-worker behind him. "It's pretty malty but the caramel undertones really bring it together."

"I'll take it! We'll each have one" she smiles with an excited hiccup as her hands fall underneath her chin. She leans over to Sherryl "You'll love it! This is the one I was telling you about."

"I'm willing to try it." Sherryl looks back at Carol hesitantly.

"It's eight for both—tab or close out?" he focuses in on the register looking away from the girls.

"Close out please!" Carol responds as she digs through her purse for her credit card.

"I'll bring it right out ladies."

The two make their way over to an indoor table for four. The place is nearly empty, excluding two other tables.

"So anyway, I just really need a happy Saturday night," Carol groans too Sherryl. Sherryl tries to recapture her earlier engagement as she shifts her focus to Carol from the two paintings behind her. The first painting depicts a fox in a forest. The second a collection of books stacked with care, eyeglasses perched on the top book. She feels bemused by them and their ability to seem ill-suited next to each other yet comforting, like how holding hands feel as they intertwine.

"I'm sure tonight will be just what you need" she responds trying to not sound patronizing. She offers a soft smile to bring Carol to a genuine ease.

"Here you ladies go" the pony-tail man says, avoiding eye-contact as he lowers their drinks to the table. Carol brings the glass closer to her face, taking in the aroma while closing her eyes, just letting herself live. She takes a drink and the sweetness reminds her of a polished acoustic until the caramel tangs brings her back to the moment.

"You're right" she smiles back in agreement.

The two remain silent for a moment as they admire their surroundings—Sherryl at the perplexing images, Carol at the two remaining tables. The first table, closer to them, is populated by a larger group, a mix of three men and two women. Carol overhears as one of the guys is sharing a story about his athletic endeavors much to the pleasure of most of the group. She notices that one of the women seems a bit more pensive and agitated than the rest of the group, with her arms around her chest and eyes lingering toward the door like she wants to leave. The second table, though, intrigues Carol: a man sits alone with his eyes as intense as a blacksmith, sharpening the words coming out of his book. He never looks up as he brings his glass to his lips, taking back his drink while his eyes remain focused. He's nearing the end of his book, but another is on the table, loaded for whenever he's finished grinding through the first.

"Carol" says Sherryl, snapping her out of a trance "What are you doing? You've been staring at that guy for the last 3 minutes!"

With her cheeks a bit red, Carol takes another drink. She looks up after putting her drink down as if contemplating the flavors but really, she is trying to regain some composure. Carol rests her chin into her left palm staring back at her mysterious scholar.

"It's just—who reads at a brewery? So strange!" she whispers with more excitement in her voice than she intends. Sherryl's eyes tighten at the corners as she takes in Carol.

"You think he's cute" she says, lifting her eyebrows as she emphasizes "cute," while Carol takes another sip to reduce the chance of Sherryl identifying her red cheeks. "Go talk to him," Sherryl's tone brightens as the word "him" lingers around Carol.

"You know what—I will," Carol giggles like a dream and stands up. She wonders if this is the start of that adventure she is craving. She stands still for a bit too long before finally remembering quite how to walk. With each step her apparent discomfort becomes more noticeable, like a baby deer finding its way. She grows closer and closer, though the avid reader still has not looked up from his book, even as she is standing right in front of him.

"I like your shirt" she says while running her second finger down his sternum. She's never done that before yet felt drawn to. The buzz of his heartbeat makes him feel like it blends with the cotton of his soft navy-blue t-shirt, blurring lines of red and blue in his head as he sees her for the first time.

"Oh God! Why did I do that?" she yelps before bursting into an uncomfortable laugh. His concentration has finally been broken, and his face looks like he is in a state of confusion and unease. "I'm so sorry!" She tightens her fist into balls and leans back in discomfort. "I don't know what I'm doing, gah!"

"Oh, uh... You're fine" he says, his face relaxes into a light smile though his eyebrows are asking her something.

"I'm just gonna leave," she points back to her table where Sherryl is smirking as if she doesn't want to burst out of her chair with laughter.

"No, seriously. You were fine," he lets out a soft chuckle in a hope to make her stay. "I'm Joel by the way," his words hit the floor around her ankles. She trails off, though, before realizing that she could have stayed. Joel returns to his book with a mild stare on the words, his mind stuck on the few she said. Across the bar, Carol arrives back to her table. Sherryl bites her tongue as Carol sits back down.

"Not a word" Carol points at Sherryl. Sherryl finally succumbs to her laughter. Carol reduces the redness in her cheeks with a sip of her drink. She looks back to Joel's table and he's disappeared. Carol wonders if that could have been the new adventure she is looking for.

A QUIET MAN

Midnight blue wraps better around him than most people's hands fit gloves. The silver wings attached over his heart, though not currently being worn, radiate from his chest. The young man smiles with his eyes as he looks out over the Charlotte Douglas Airport atrium. He walks over to a standing table to rest his arms and he places down his brownish-red bag. He crosses his hands into the inside bends of his elbows and presses his body closer to the table.

A mother is scolding one of her children while a younger one follows behind like a little duck. The older crosses his arms and sits on the ground, his tiny face growing red like a plum. The mother squats and raises the troublesome child over her shoulder. The younger puts her thumb in her mouth as she looks up at her troublemaker of a brother. The tiny plum boy's tears begin to stream down his face as the mother carries him off, her little duck quick to follow behind. He hears the mother address the little duck as they pass, "Sweetie, you are four now. You have to stop sucking on your thumb." The man smirks at the scene as the little duck is quick to pull her thumb out of her mouth.

"Last call for Flight 2048 to Dallas," a voice over the airport intercom says. The man looks up, though he just arrived from his flight. North

Carolina is home now. The man grabs his phone to check on the weather and build his plan for the remainder of the week. He receives a text and it says it's from Mom,

So proud of you! I know you just saw me, but congratulations again on graduating from your training. I'll visit you soon sweetie.

"Can I get you anything sir?" a waitress appears as if out of thin air, startling him. His eyes grow as wide as an egg but return to normal as he catches the phone that popped out of his hands when she startled him. The standing table is outside of whatever restaurant she belongs to.

"No, thanks," the man says without much movement of his mouth. He looks down at the table, embarrassed that she caught him off guard.

"Okay, well if you change your mind my name is Bennie," she says lifting her shoulders up as she says her name.

"I'll just be on my way," the man turns in the opposite direction and begins on his way out of the airport while trying to save face. Bennie stares with a trace of bewilderment at him, holding her small notepad.

His phone vibrates alerting him of a text: his driver will pick him up in the next hour and give him a ride to his new location. He stares back out over the atrium. He notices an older gentleman with a brown fedora is swinging on a rocking chair while reading the newspaper. After he passes out of the terminal gates into the baggage area he grabs a seat looking out over everyone else leaving. The world is full of so many different stories.

A little finger presses against his outer left knee. The man stares down and sees the little duck child, her hair in ponytails protruding from both sides of her head. Without a second's hesitation, his head feels heavy as he lifts it up. His eyes feel dizzy after looking side to side for her mother; she's nowhere in his sight. He stands up, hoping that doing so will somehow reveal her to be somewhere that he just isn't able to see sitting down. A small gulp erupts from the back of his throat as the unease cuts at the air like a tiny toy airplane engine, until the little girl speaks.

"You don't talk much, mister," the little duck says, still prodding at his left knee.

"I don't," he mutters and shoos her hand away. "Please stop that. Where is your mother?" he asks, looking for anyone that can help in this situation.

"I... I... I don't know." she says, both of their hearts starting to crack as she stops speaking. He almost tells her to keep poking his left knee if it will stop her from crying. "Can you find her?" she looks up at him "I walked with the wrong lady. Her shirt was like my mama's... and now I don't where my ma..." her voice begins to crack, so she stops.

"We'll find her" he tells her trying his best to not sound cold; talking has always made him uneasy. He isn't even sure how to talk to kids, but he is really trying with her, his voice even offering a bit of brightness that not many have ever heard.

"I thought you were a police man," she pauses and wipes her eyes with her gray sweater. "Cause you're all blue..."

"I am— Air Force, though," the man lets her know and pats her head once to console her. "We'll find your mom." An energy flicks on in the little girl, drying up her tears as she smiles up at the man.

"Thank you, mister. I'm Chrissy," she stretches out her tiny hand to him, and her back arches to the shape of the first letter of her name.

"Jaxton" he shakes her hand, treating her with the same respect he would any adult.

"You're kind of weird," Chrissy says, tilting her head to the left and offering a light laugh.

Bending at his knees to be lower with her, Jaxton puts his index and thumb about an inch apart and squinches his eye "Just a little bit." Chrissy erupts into a laugh bigger than her, forgetting if only for a moment that she's lost. Jaxton begins to weigh the next steps in his mind. His head swivels both ways, the same way a hungry turtle would, searching for a nearby TSA agent or information booth.

"You still don't talk much, mister," Chrissy prodding his left knee again. She already forgot that he asked her not too.

"Not my super power," Jaxton grabs his bag and throws it onto his back. They begin to walk back to the terminals in hopes of finding an information booth. They can search for Chrissy in the system to find her mother. The little duck follows right behind, keeping up at a jog pace with her little legs. Jaxton slows down to let her catch up, watching with a sense of concern. He fears that the mother left on a flight without Chrissy. They grow closer to a booth outside of the terminal area.

He wishes in his mind that if Chrissy's flight left with her family on it, he could help in some way. He remembers a red cape from his childhood. An image of him flying up to the plane while carrying Chrissy floats across his mind. The crowd on the plane erupts into cheer and applause as he boards the plane. Chrissy's mother bursts from out of her seat. She peels down to the end of the airplane aisle to embrace Chrissy, ignoring the "Please Remain Seated" neon lights that were flickering above while her older brother looks like a puppy whose owner just returned home after a week-long vacation from his seat. Wagging his imaginary tail as he watches from his seat on his knees.

Jaxton shakes his head to break the stream of thought. Surely the mother would never board the plane without Chrissy, nor could he fly.

Jaxton and Chrissy approach the airport information desk.

"Hello," Jaxton nods at the woman attendant, she smiles back though she doesn't want to. "This little girl has gotten separated from her mother," the attendant continues to stare, not wanting the conversation to go any further. Jaxton's voice starts to shake as his tone begins to dance with a bit of a flame due to the women's lack of concern, "We need to find some information on this little girl so she can get back to her mother." His voice settles to a lighter whisper like a bonfire at the end of a night as he finishes his sentence.

The woman turns to Chrissy and barely tries to hide a small roll of her eyes, "What's your full name sweetie?" trying to sound nicer than she is.

"Chrissy um, um, Sherman..." she whispers like she wants to hide. She's unsure if the woman is even capable of help. Chrissy backs a couple paces away from the counter wanting to run away. Her eyes begin to water.

"It's okay sweetie," the woman says, as if she just became more aware of her presence. "We're going to get you back to your mom," she leans over the counter separating them, trying to invite Chrissy back closer to her. Chrissy's tiny body eases like a breath leaving the body on a cold winter day. As she takes a step closer back to the attendant and Jaxton, a stranger's hand grabs her from around the waist.

Chrissy's eyes grow tight. She shrieks as she notices the weight of her own feet no longer bearing any mass, the hands wrapped around her were not of someone known to her. Her shriek is a dot in comparison to the sound of a woman's voice in the distance. A blur of emotions come screeching out of the terminal area. Chrissy's mother's face appears from out of the blended emotions. The little boy, tucked away in his mother's right arm, looks distraught as he pieces the puzzles of the scene together in his mind. A look of anguish sits upon his face as he realizes what is happening.

"Chrissy!" her mother screams, the sound pierces through the airport like open fire and causes patrons to turn and watch. Chrissy's mother runs toward her little duck with her arms outstretched. Chrissy reaches back for her mother though the stranger is pulling her in the opposite direction. "Someone help my baby!"

The information attendant grabs at the phone "TSA we have a kidnapping in motion," her fingers trembling as she realizes she needs to still dial. Finally finding the right combination she barks with more authority "TSA we have a kidnapping in motion! I repeat kidnapping in motion!" A gurgled response can be heard from the telephone.

Jaxton is frozen in disbelief, if only for a moment. He dissolves like an icy rock in a pot after hearing Chrissy's mom shout, his legs responding to the situation before his brain can compute. He keeps pace with the kidnapper as Chrissy's face begs him to get her out of this nightmare, her open mouth offering nothing more than terrified sobs. As Jaxton gets within striking distance, the piss-poor excuse of a man that started the chase tosses Chrissy back and out from underneath his arm. Jaxton slides like water pouring in a glass, catching Chrissy and placing her safely on the ground. He kicks up from his slide and onto his feet still in sprint, hitting maximum overdrive as he leaps out at the kidnapper. He swipes at the kidnapper's left leg, grabbing a hold of his shoelace. The kidnapper hops on one foot before he rolls forward and onto his back. Jaxton lunges at the man as if he were a bear whose cub is in danger and, with one fist, delivers a knockout punch. The kidnapper's body goes limp. A crowd of onlookers stare in silent awe at Jaxton. Chrissy quivers a couple paces away, her face caught between a pensive smile and someone who got lost at a funeral.

A few seconds of disbelief are shared by them all. A round man whose shirt doesn't quite cover his belly drops his silver rolling bag and raises a fist as he cheers "Hurrah! What a champ!" A select few of the onlookers offer a light clap as if it were a quiet sporting venue. The majority continue to make their way towards their flights—they don't want to be late. Chrissy's mother is able to make her way to Chrissy and she plucks her little duck up from off the ground. Whispers are shared between the two, as the tears from both blend with each other. Jaxton rolls off the man, still motionless, and relaxes his elbows over his knees. He takes a deep breath, though not allowing the man to leave his view even for a single moment despite being knocked out. TSA finally arrives. The man begins to wake as they place his drowsy body into handcuffs. None of them acknowledge Jaxton. As they get the man onto his feet and walking away, a little duck pokes again at Jaxton's left knee.

"Mr. Jaxton" Chrissy says "You're my hero." Chrissy giggles through the tear stains on her cheeks. "I wish you had a cape!" The image of a bright red cape from his childhood floats across Jaxton's mind. She runs back to her mother, turning just before she reaches her. She pinches her thumb and index finger together, "But you're still a little weird." Jaxton smiles and nods as he makes his way outside to find his ride.

Alan J. Chambers

BOOK II – THE STORM

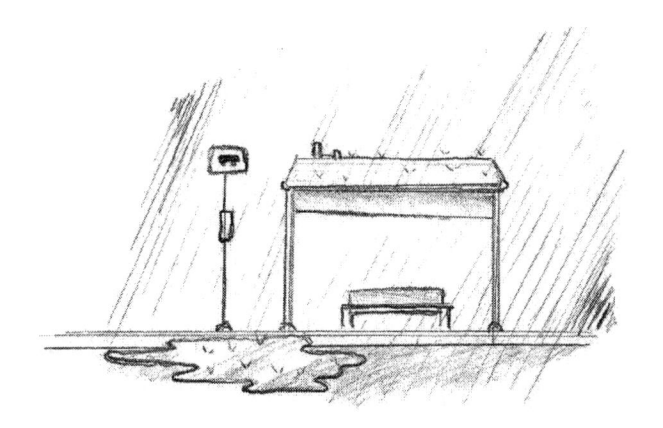

A LETTER TO MR. THORNE

Dear. Mr. Thorne

    I never learned your first name. I think the letters rolling from her tongue would have punctured it like an iron spike into a tire, rolling down the street with no car attached. I could never ask her what your name was - maybe she would've written it down if I asked. Her eyes would fill with tears as she scribbled, scrawling out the letters as if the pen were a dagger in her hand. I'd feel tempted to say it aloud, to make it real - I never could. She'd look at me with her eyes strained, bracing for impact - daring me to say your name.

That letter-forged blade would have cut me too, knowing that you loved her first, that you had her first, that you held her longer, that you made her believe in love, and that you married her. I couldn't do any of that—thanks to you.

You killed her, man. Why? What did you do to her?

Did you seduce another woman in the bed you shared with her? Did you push one of your damn fists against her (You better hope I don't find out if you ever did.)? Maybe something a little subtler. Did you just talk to other women? No intent of ever pursuing them but continuing to ignite the flames of her jealousy that has now licked us both. Maybe you told her you never loved her in the heat of an argument, speaking the words and then realizing you couldn't eat them back up, leaving a vomit-like stain in her brain that just won't get clean no matter how many times she has scrubbed you away.

I know you kept her house, and all the gifts you both received from your wedding. At least the house wasn't in her hometown. This place is already haunted enough for her. I had to sit with her as she would sift through crowds everywhere we went, to make sure there was no trace of you. Seeing the smallest particle of dust that you may have left meant that I couldn't stay in that location with her. I had to keep moving and searching with her, while having no idea who you were or what you're like.

You still have her trapped, you know. I loved her more than you ever did. I know that's true because I loved her even after the mess that you left her in. She was a hurricane after you. I was merely a bystander who got wrapped into her. I also know she never actually loved me back. She wanted to, she really did. But you took that away from her. It's like she's still locked up in your trap. I grabbed the key and set her free—she just still couldn't see that she could move on from your trap.

You killed her Mr. Thorne.

Worst Wishes,
Terrance

I WANT A SAD SUNDAY
(PART II - INTJ)

The ceiling fan swings round and around while I watch with eyes wide open. I fear one of the blades losing its natural place and swinging at me. I just need for things to stay the way they are. But I'm tired of feeling alone. Eternity courses through my bones before I jolt myself like lightning out of bed. The soft navy-blue T-shirt I wore the night before is on the ground by my bed. I shiver, why did I forget to put it in the basket? I never forget to put things where they are supposed to be. That girl from the bar last night threw me out of my normal patterns.

"You're fine Joel. It's just a shirt." I whisper to no one. I undress my other half and turn the corner into my bathroom.

A steamy vapor forms within moments of the shower turning on. My mind drifts into an obscure thought of clouds, lifted to a place where I'm not quite me. I float along the heavens, as if I believe that I belong. After many minutes pass I fracture through the mist like a new idea.

I do need a change— I just don't know what.

I hear the swoosh of a door opening, I crank my neck and steady my footing as I fear to lose it. I grab a towel and wrap it around my waist as I set off like I'm walking on needles. My footsteps are lingering as I tiptoe out of the bathroom leaving little puddles behind, they'll evaporate eventually anyways.

"Hello?" I ask, "Is anyone there?"

The wind chimes in but he does not answer. Why, oh why won't he answer... The patio is untouched as the open-door stares. I feel fear that a whole new life is outside of that door. I grow closer as I realize that I hope that's true.

With a spurious caution I continue towards the patio. As I inch closer and closer the wind from outside beats against my chest like an old tribal calling, like I'm finally home.

I can't fathom what could await me out there, but I know it's where I need to be. Foliage becomes clear, the sky a crisp gray. One step out the door, now two...

The door behind me closes like a flower hitting the ground. I wait for something, anything else to happen. My breath is visible as I see it float like little clouds in front of me.

I feel empty as I realize there's nothing out here for me. I reach out to the countertop on my patio and grab an unfiltered cigarette. I walked through the door but there was no adventure out here for me. What more did I need to do? I finish the cigarette in eight puffs.

I go back inside following the disappointment. The ceiling fan swings round and around while I watch with eyes closed shut.

ROSE

A crew of five employees circle around me. My eyes shift to my glass of water. I don't want to rest my eyes on any of theirs. Their identical smiles and black shirts inscribed with "Steakhouse" make my heart panic more than it should.

Happy Birthday to You

Happy Birthday to You

Happy Birthday Dear Terrance

Happy Birthday to You.

"Thank you all!" I say like a sheep, wanting to return to my flock. My fingers fidget underneath the table. I beg them to walk away while sipping the water from my glass so I don't have to keep speaking to them. The tallest of the group, a woman, whose smile is a bit too big for her face understands.

"Enjoy the rest of your night you two!" the tall woman says, and I wish I had read the name on her badge. She guides the two younger employees away with her hands on their shoulders. The other two singers understood to walk away on their own.

"Why do you enjoy torturing me Rose?" I put down the glass of water. My voice sounds closer to a wolf than a sheep, but the tone isn't sharp, like their fangs. I smile at Rose and place my left index finger across my lips as I stare across the table upon her beauty. Her hair is a light brown, like a sweet honey. I feel myself getting stuck in between everything that rests underneath her honey. My heart reaches across the table, telling her to come closer, as she pushes the black thick-rimmed glasses closer to her eyes. She scrunches her face when the glasses feel just right against it, and everything inside of me scrunches the same way.

"I like to see you squirm babe," Rose lets me know. She circles the top of her wine glass as she smiles at me like a bumble bee. I worry of her sting but she buzzes closer to me. She stands up from her chair and slides over to me, coming to a rest in my lap. She strokes the short trim hair above my head. Each finger feels like a gentle wave of water. I've never felt the freedom of an ocean against my knees, but I know that this is better. "Are you having a good birthday, my boy?"

"You're my favorite person," my mouth says words that I didn't even know existed but were more true than anything I've ever said in my life. "You're my favorite person to ever exist. Ever." I smile as the truth of the words make me feel like I just learned how to walk.

After the words march out of my mouth, just as they are ordered to do, I stare at her. She smiles like the words were gifts from every birthday she's ever had. I don't think she knew she could feel that happy in one single moment.

"You don't mean that..." she places her head against my shoulder, sinking deeper into me. She wants me to tell her more, I must oblige. I wrap my arms around her entire body and squeeze with a gentle tug of my hands. With every fiber of my body she feels my warmth and knows I am deeply and madly in love with her. I place my finger underneath her chin, disturbing her rest against my shoulder, and place my lips against her forehead. She knows that I am safety and that she will never feel alone again. Her eyes are a cool blue and she looks like she just said the word 'love' as she leans back onto my shoulder.

"I hope you know I'm going to marry you someday." I say.

"I'm... I'm not ready for that Terrance..." she pulls her head out of the pocket of my shoulder and her eyes grow a bit too wide. She puts her hand over my heart. She doesn't want to break it, but she knows hers isn't ready.

"I'm not saying tomorrow, and I'm not saying in the next three years. I'm saying whenever you are ready to take that step with me, I plan to marry you." I say, and I feel myself breathe. I don't think I have ever noticed how clean it feels until I met her.

"Thank you... You're my favorite person too Terrance... Just so you know..." she leans back into my shoulder, and I see her smile even though she tries to face away from me. I let her rest.

"Can I get you two anything else?!" the tall waitress returns, and this time I catch that her badge reads Layla. She shifts the entire energy of the moment as her eyes stick on us—she's ready to collect her tip and go home.

"No... We're fine. Can I get the check please?" I stroke along Rose's left shoulder and feel a light prick against my palm from her outfit. Her body feels rooted against mine, as she doesn't shift at all while I reach for my wallet. Rose feels safe with me.

A week has passed from my birthday and water is falling from the sky. The cold drips of water rings through our ears as we listen from the living room couch. Her depression begins to creep out from her closet and press against the bottom of the couch. It keeps pushing until it climbs into the couch with us. The air around us suddenly feels colder and she quivers. Her presence changes as it seems she lost some color when she shivered.

"I can't sit here." Rose's eyes scan the room as if she is expecting someone to be hiding behind the rest of her furniture. When she stands I notice a patch of dry roses where she was sitting. I reach down to the maroon roses with a faint hope to recover them and the petals crumble. I stare back to her with a face of remorse, hoping Rose doesn't think I made it worse. Her eyes are a naive green, hiding rain from a forgotten forest. They drift to the window staring outside. "Let's go, I can't sit here." She grabs her keys and my hand with the other, dragging us both outside into the rain.

"Where are we trying to go Rose?" I ask as the rain begins to wash over us both.

"I don't know. You need to pick." She hands me the keys and I get the feeling she isn't even talking to me. Her words seem hollow and rehearsed like she's said them time and time again to a former lover. I bite my tongue as I start the car, nervous that I might be right. I decide to take her to our favorite spot— the book store where we both felt like we could be alone but together. Our minds allowed to drift in other worlds while she would lay firmly in my lap.

We don't speak during the drive as she continues to watch the rain. I brush my hand over her thigh and she leans against me. Her eyes close and I feel assured that she still feels safe with me. As I park I move my hand from her thigh and can feel another prick, like a thorn, against my palm like the other day.

"Please don't ever let me go Terrance..." she says so quietly underneath the hush of the car engine winding down.

"I promise." I smile as I stare at her and know that I will never want to hold onto anyone else. When she exits the car, again I notice rose petals in her seat, though the color is a bit more vibrant this time. Maybe I am making her better. I reach out and they disintegrate once more. The rain beings to pour down harder.

"Terrance. Hurry up, I'm freezing." With crossed arms Rose walks to the entrance, paces ahead of me while her eyes are scanning everything around her. She's always looking for him, her ex-husband. Maybe I'm not enough.

"Rose... I'm never going to be him. In anyway." I stop to say, standing in the rain as she stands beneath the entrance's canopy. "I will never abandon you the way he did."

"Oh. Okay," she says refusing to look at me. "We're just for fun anyways. This isn't even real." The words are as sharp as a thorn as they open me at the seams and although she said them so soft, they rip me apart so hard.

"Rose... do you even like me?" I ask, she grabs my hand and drags me inside, toying with me like a child's game. I don't know what she wants from me. As I stare back to where I was standing I notice the purple petals of my favorite flower, a calla lily, have fallen behind me left floating away in the rain with her rose petals. She loves me not.

Alan J. Chambers

THE CAGE OF (POVERTY, FEAR & MONOTONY)

The freedom I can't seem to find always appears to be right outside my window. A sliver of doubt sneaks into my mind as my feet find their way around in the dark to guide me to the front door. My fingers latch around the faded gold doorknob, I pause for a second to decide whether outside is really where I want to go. With little effort, it twists and opens to an adventure outside.

The night is a cool blue with a misty dew glazing over the brown lawn. I walk out onto the driveway and I slide my hand over the front of the hollow aluminum frame of my '90 Honda Accord. She is a sight for only my sore eyes, no one else ever cared enough to give her a second glance. No one else ever wants to give her a chance in life, so I guess we have that in common. I bump into the the right-side mirror of the car with my left elbow, and being the junker car she is, the mirror falls off with little resistance, colliding to the ground with a quick crack, as if a whip had been lashed in its direction. The broken glass settles around it in a circular formation. The glass causes a scurry in the creatures from underneath the trashcans to return from where they came. I shudder from the sound but try to laugh to ease the mild tension that is forming in my head. I hear the squeak of my neighbors' screen doors opening behind me, and I turn to face the front door of my house to hide my embarrassment. I sigh, admitting that I want more out of a car than it being able to normally turn on. I want one that will make, not just my classmates, but my teachers turn their heads when I drive by. Maybe someday...

This is not the home my mind wants to imagine would start tonight's adventure. The doors are not a bright, welcoming red, but instead a worn brown, tired as an unraveling sweater washed too many times. This small house will never be my home. I need to make a new home, one that doesn't reek of opened orange pill bottles and stale bread. We always have to buy the bread on clearance, and it always spoils before we can finish it. My mother is out cold in her room from medication, unaware that I am about to roam the streets.

She couldn't stop me anyways, I felt a hunger to see the world outside. That hunger always makes me want to get better with everything I do. I know she never chose for this to happen in her life—her getting sick just happened, and we just didn't have anyone else to help but I still want to achieve my dreams. I swore to her that I will make a name for myself— though right now it's my job to tend to her. I start every morning with the same routine: clean the dishes, cook my mother's meals for the day, prepare her daily doses of medication, start the dryer, fight back tears, serve my mother her food and pills, take out the trash, fold the clothes from the dryer, breakdown in the laundry room where no one else can hear me, prepare my lunch, walk to school. The afternoon's tasks are more tedious, but I don't want to think about them right now. I know though that I am going to help us escape from this place at some point. A tinge of guilt fills my heart as I worry over whether I'll hurt my mom by wanting more than she is able to give me. I hope she'll forgive me— I want to get far in life for her anyways.

I put my headphones in, my hood up, and my shoes lead me away onto the damp concrete with no real direction in mind. Just a feeling:

there is somewhere calling me, somewhere I am meant to be.

I've never really been anywhere worth returning to, but it is always nice to try and look for such a destination. Tonight, seems like as great a time as any to find such a place. The lights the night possess have a way of making me feel more alive than anything else could. I turn down Georgia Avenue, a friendly corner that I would occasionally drive by in my beat-down Accord, but now it seems dim and uninviting. It isn't enough to stop me; the street is getting my company whether it wants me to go down it or not. And although I grimace with each step pounding against Georgia Avenue, I refuse to be swayed by the fear that resides inside of me and I continue forward.

The houses I walk along are the ones I wish I had been able to grow up in. A warm and sunny orange house with a huge bay window where a family could look out caught my eye the most. I stop to look it up and down. It is a two-story house with no lights on, so I assume the family must be out. They must be the type of family that could afford to go out to a fancy restaurant. The top of the house is shaped like a triangle with a brick chimney on the left corner. The front lawn is a bright green, even this late at night, and with a miniature waterfall that the homeowners must leave on all the time as the stream whispers a gentle tune to complement the still and quiet night. The front door is a soft silver that welcomes all to comfort, as if it would never hurt them. I imagine the laughter of a child that lives there, he can know the joy of this world before he learns one day of the pain that resides outside as well. He will hold beautiful memories that he can go back to in his times of pain. Whenever he is feeling down a crackling image of orange and silver will surround him, and he will remember the love of his parents. My mother tries I remind myself but working so hard is probably what got her so sick in the first place. I just keep staring in wonder at that house hoping that hours are passing, so I can feel like no one will make me ever leave. This house is what I want out of my life.

I've spent so many days living behind my own shadow. "I'm done being in the dark!" I scream, though no one is around to hear me and the sound fades and dies. As the last echo dissipates, the street light I am standing underneath goes out. I stop and stand in place while I shake my head with the fear of the dark inching upon me. The dark reminds me that maybe I don't deserve that life I want. No cars are out tonight despite it being a Saturday. At least I think it's Saturday, it might be Sunday—I always lose track of time when I linger inside my house's four walls for too long. Everything outside of my home always felt so foreign my entire life but I don't want to feel that way anymore. The pleasant orange of my dream home turns into a blaze of fire inside me—I want to burn down my past life, break down the walls that trapped me and let more life in. Rebuild.

I hear a dog barking and the sensation rings in my ears. The dog has a savage looking mouth with frightening canines that hold saliva weaved throughout the teeth. The race begins with me falling backwards onto my rear, as this beast's appearance caught me dumbfounded. I run in the opposite direction of the terror behind me, a sense of heat burning like little embers on my back as I can feel it gaining on me. I sprint out of Georgia Avenue across to an empty, unnamed street in hope of finding a better escape route among the restaurant alleyways. As I approach the sidewalk it catches my eye: a chained gate that lays between an alleyway caught between an apartment complex and a pizza parlor. It isn't much, but there is no way this dog can climb up the fencing to follow me.

As I start climbing to escape I feel it. A deep pain ran across my backside as I realize that the maniacal dog has managed to jump at the same time as me and has taken a chunk of my jeans with it. I throw myself onto the ground from the top of the fence but I land uncomfortably on my left ankle during the impact, I try to shake it off but each step feels painful. Metal wiring is all that separates me from the snarling beast at this point. My arms shake at my side as she stares at me through the fence.

"You happy with yourself? You wretched dog!" I say trying to disperse the fear from inside me. She appears content with herself as she shakes her head in an angry response, the fabric of my jeans still in her mouth. I reach to my right buttock and feel the cold cloth that is my underwear. The sound of pennies hitting the ground draws me back to the dog. I look down to see my change fall to the ground as the dog tore apart a couple dollar bills. I didn't have much to begin with, but the little I had is now gone and there is nothing I can do about it.

Cold sweat forms over my brow as I pace along the outskirts of the fence while contemplating my next move. The wallet, and all it had contained, is destroyed at this point and the dog eyes me with a menacing display of her canines. I feel helpless as she peers into my eyes as if she is more than a dog and she stares straight through me. Distraught by my unfair advantage of climbing the fence, the dog meanders away, though she continues to maniacally look back to where I am. I stare for as long as I can at the ever-decreasing ferocious dot that is nearly gone. I sink down onto my knees and pound with the bottom of my fists at the ground. The dog came out of nowhere and I hadn't been able to do anything but run away. I wipe my nose and eyes as I lift myself off the ground to better gage my surroundings. If she comes back, she will not get the better of me. I refuse to let the fear she creates in me cage me here.

If the coast is clear then it will be easy to make a clear break back home. I pull off my shoes and place the shoelaces in my mouth as I pull upward on the fence. I am on full alert listening to any potential sounds that may signal she is still here. Upon reaching the top of the fence I straddle one leg over the top of the fence with a shoe in hand. With a lethargic toss I watch my shoe leave my hand and it seems that any hope I have is thrown with it. My shoe seems to hang around in the air, forever approaching the ground for an infinite amount of time. The dog is salivating, watching my shoe spinning closer and closer to her mouth. With the bat of my eyelids I realize this moment may be my only chance to get away.

I throw my other leg over the remainder of the fence and take off in the opposite direction. It doesn't take long for her to realize she has been duped, and she advances towards me. I can sense her presence all around me and I know she is gaining me. I feel her breath against my ankles for a moment. She goes for the bite and she manages to pull off a bit of hair from my ankle.

I think of the orange home and I let that fire take a hold of me. I am going to get out of this. I will get what I want out of this life—fear will not stop me. I let my breath settle into a pace and the muscles in my leg begin to pump stronger than most machines could ever dare to. I refuse to let her catch me. I must give this chase everything I got.

A siren makes a whirring sound from a distance away. I see lights approaching from up ahead in the distance. This must be death waiting to welcome me. I can't feel my legs anymore. I look down to make sure I am still running. They are pumping against the street though I feel numb and the bottom of my pants are tattered. The lights grow closer. The sound remains distinct and is becoming much louder. I turn around to see how close the dog is and to my satisfaction it has backed off into the other direction with the approaching lights and sounds. I ease up a bit from my sprint and see a car honking as it approaches me. The front seat driver rolls down his window and streams of smoke poke its way out. A fit of coughing develops from the back of the car. I wave the smoke out from in front of me to dispense the musty stench and the driver lets out a horrid cackle.

"Ya need a ride kid?" he asks. "I got room for one more." I look past him and see his other two passengers. The front seat passenger wears a baseball cap while sporting a brooding demeanor. His arms are crossed against his chest and he doesn't turn in my direction. In the backseat a petite female with curly red hair is struggling out of her seatbelt to get a glimpse at what they had stopped for. A gray beanie sits on top of the driver's head. His hair is a shaggy brown that pops out of the back corners of his cap. He keeps both hands on the steering wheel while looking at me. I have never seen anyone drive with gloves on until now. His gloves are ragged and have holes throughout. Most of the finger holes seem to be missing from them. The three of them don't quite match the car. I can't depict what brand the car is and the car appears to be stripped of any decals that would classify it. The color is a sleek platinum gray and it glistens in the moonlight.

"Are ya deaf kid? Do you want a ride or not?" he says. "I'm not gonna ask again."

"No, yes please!" I say, "Please don't leave me out here."

"Well you can ride in back with Smiley here," gesturing to his passenger, "and Patty will move to the front with me"

"Oh sweet! You're finally gonna let me ride shotty?" says Patty in a shrill voice, "By the way, what's your name kid?" she crawls over the center console to the front while Smiley opens his door to move to the

The Balloon in the Storm

back.

"I, uh, my name's David." I say, not wanting to divulge my entire identity. It is in fact my middle name, so it isn't a complete lie.

"Well I'm Hank, unless you wanna get left out here, get in the damn car."

"Yes sir" I say while jumping into the back on the driver's side.

"Don't give me that "sir" nonsense, I said my name's Hank!"

"Alright my bad, it's a habit."

He drives off before I have a chance to put on my seatbelt and I stumble into his seat. Hank and Patty chuckle at my embarrassment, though Smiley remains glued to his window. The night appears to be ending as dawn is arriving with the promise of sunlight in a couple hours. Until then we are stuck in this twilight with glimmers of the sun poking out. Hank keeps driving onward though he never asked me where I want to go. I feel exhausted and am too thankful to ask where we are headed. I merely want to relax for a moment. I close my eyes and let the air of the car enter my lungs. I can't believe my luck that I have been saved by these strangers. Smiley speaks to me though he doesn't change his view.

"Why were you out there?" he asks without any traces of emotion.

"I don't really know... I just went out for a walk."

"This late at night? That's pretty stupid."

"Yeah I guess so, but it seemed like a nice night for such a thing."

"Nothing good happens after three A.M."

"It's not like I was planning on being out past then! I was being chased," I say, growing disgruntled by his apathetic tone.

"Yeah we saw you running for your life."

"Well, thanks anyways."

Patty stops her whispers into Hank's ears to comment, "Smiles, stop pestering him! Be nice." She has her arms around Hank while he remains dead set focused on the road in front of him.

I begin again, "Why are you guys out here anyways? Besides you're the one who just said nothing good happens after three A.M."

"We do this every night."

"You all drive out this way every night?"

"Yup, that's what I said."

"Don't you all have jobs or something?"

"Nope."

"How do you possibly afford to do this every night? And this, this is a pretty nice car to just be cruising around in."

"We've just been borrowing it for a while, might not give it back though, or I guess might not have too." he says while turning to face towards me. I finally understand why they call him Smiley as he bears a set of perfect, white teeth. It strikes me that there is something hidden beyond his smile—but in this moment, it seems genuine. I look over the rest of his facial features and catch a glimpse of his eyes. They are a refined blue and yet I feel as if in that second I caught a glimpse of the pain that he hides behind his smile. His eyes are bloodshot, and they appear to be sunken into his head more than they should be. I turn away as my stomach gets uneasy with him staring at me.

"Leave the kid alone, he was already being chased by big ol' Lilly tonight" says Patty as she turns to face the back

"Just having a little fun back here" says Smiley not hiding his guilty smile.

"Don't you worry David, they borrow the car from their fathers. They're kinda like doctors or something so they always drop the cash for these two" Patty nods her head like she has said those words before.

"It's fine, like uhh Smiley said, it was all in fun," I say, almost believing myself.

Smiley drops another grin towards me for defending him. I didn't actually look back at him but I could feel his stare burning against my back.

"Why do you all come out here every night?"

"What else do we have to do?" says Smiley.

"Well if your parents will pay for anything why not do something else?" Smiley sinks back into his chair as no one has ever asked him that.

"I guess we just never thought there was anything *better* to do. I don't know, it doesn't really matter what else I'd want to do. Does it?" Smiley begins to stroke his left arm as he contemplates.

We sit in silence for what feels like an hour. I am still uncertain of where we are going and at this point I am too afraid to ask.

"I used to watch trees grow when I was really little." says Smiley who is again staring out the window with a despondent demeanor: "I would sit for hours on the grass and just watch them for days on end until I would be called inside. They always found a way to keep growing and shaping around whatever was around them. I wanted to be like that. But I don't think I am," Smiley turns towards me and I stare back.

"But maybe you can be."

"This might be weird to say... But you remind of those trees." His eyes lost that sad undertone for a minute. He turns slowly back to the window. Dawn is now upon us and I am now aware that we have driven somewhere onto the eastern side of the city. Patty has fallen asleep while Hank remains determined in his driving.

"I live just up ahead, if you wouldn't mind letting me out." I say, knowing I am lying and unsure of how to get home from here.

"Hey David, you should join us again. We always start at a little orange house on Georgia Avenue." says Hank. I shudder as I realize which house they were talking of.

"Yeah, Smiley's parents left us with it, and we normally take off around 11 PM"

"I'll try to join you all soon"

"Like Smiley said, we do this every night"

With that, they are off back into the city. I walk over to the sidewalk and sit on the ground while crossing my arms over my legs. I reflect on the prior night. Right now, I miss my worn brown, and tired door but I don't think I want to go back. I still want more than that. I no longer feel like myself, everything has changed and I can't go back. Am I a tree or just trapped in a cage? Only tomorrow's decisions will tell.

BABY BLUE

My telescope sat perched atop a tripod staring outside my second story apartment room. Last week, my mother gave it to me for my 15th birthday. My alarm clock showed that it was approaching ten o'clock as I admired the telescope from my bed while escaping the soul crushing heat of the outdoors.

"You've been laying in bed since 3 PM yesterday! Either get up, or I will make you get up, Charlie," mom beckoned while pounding like a wild beast against my door. An incoherent mumble of nothings showed enough vitality for her to stop. "It's about damn time, I swear Charlie, if it wasn't for your occasional fits of curiosity I don't know if you'd ever get anything done!" she growled, and I imagined her fists were throbbing red. I had no plans for the day, so I didn't understand why it was necessary for me to be up and at 'em. Besides, it was the summer! I should have been allowed to do as I pleased and not be forced to do anything by some form of authority. But I'd never been one for argument, so getting out of bed was the easier route.

After I put on my royal purple bathrobe, I exited my bedroom like a fox and made my way downstairs to the kitchen. My younger sister hadn't heard me yet while she watched her favorite over-colored kids' show, the kind that gives people seizures. I saw her smile lined all the way up to her left ear as she filled her brain with that TV fuzz. My mistake was in opening the refrigerator door. A smile like a grinning lion cub awaited me when I closed the door. I was not prepared to hear her shrill voice; she was worse than the birds at my window in the mornings.

"Big brother! What are we doing today?!"

"Hmmm, I think ignoring you is on the docket," I said.

"Mom said you have to start being nicer to me!" she beckoned.

"Great! The best way to do that is to avoid you." I said with a devilish smile.

"MOM!" she screamed while running towards mother's room. I was really gonna hear it now. I felt an energy of red fire brewing from her room as my sister filled her in on the details of the prior moment. The door opened, and she started to walk towards me while still placing earrings in her ear,

"Please, please, please could you not do this today, Charlie? I'm already two hours late for work, and I have enough on my plate there. I do not need you belittling your little sister and having her call me at work today."

"I'll try my best," I said, though I stared up to the ceiling with my fingers crossed behind my back.

"Look, I don't ask for you to do much around here, the least you could do is be nice to your sister," mom said in an attempt to guilt me.

"I don't mean anything by it," I apologized "Really, honest, I just love a little chuckle."

"I don't wanna hear it today. Just be nice!" mom said, her words sharing the same space of air as the wind from the door closing.

My little sister, Betty, who I called Button, came out of mom's room like a dog with her tail between her legs. She continued looking down until I addressed her.

"Hey Button! How about we watch a bit of your show!" Her face lit up with excitement as she dragged me to the living room sectional to watch.

The next two hours consisted of Button's laughter while I created a mini science experiment with the pillows I liked to call "Can You Suffocate Yourself With Living Room Furniture?" The findings revealed that it wasn't possible. The results showed that as a consequence you must endure eye sores from seeing every color known to man in addition to very flawed plotlines.

"Button... I need to go upstairs real quick." I said to save myself if only for a couple minutes, "I'll be right back down."

"You better be! Or I'm telling Mom you slept all day again!" she retorted. I needed a break from that show though, so it was worth the risk.

I closed my door and a sigh of relief left my lungs as I slid down the back of my door. The allure of my telescope shifted my eyes to it. It made my spirit rise along with my body. I walked closer to it in a daze, unsure of what was making my body move. I sat down on the little stand I'd recently bought for it. I knew that I couldn't look out into the stars that early, so I zoomed the lens out to look around. There was an empty landscape of dirt surrounding our apartment complex. I sat my view towards the interstate and there was a shortage of cars traveling through. I guessed everyone must have been at work. I returned my views to the surrounding dirt out of disappointment. My vision sat on a dirt hill. I made sure to take in every detail of that hill like a calligrapher writing his will. A peculiar color was coming from atop, and I zoomed in to get a better view: an antique baby blue couch in perfect condition sat abandoned.

A sense of discomfort began to fill my stomach and I wanted to vomit. There was nothing unappealing about the couch so I'm unsure why it caused that reaction. I started to throb down on the ground with a dry gag filling the air around me. After a deep breath, I was able to pick myself up. I found myself drawn to that baby blue couch even more, like it had my name written over it and it taunted me to come look. I never understood what it meant when people said that nonsense but, in that moment, I was able to empathize. It had my curiosity hooked and I felt like nothing could stop me from going out and looking at it in person.

"Hey Button, you wanna go on an adventure?" I asked.

"What?! Really, big brother?!" Button replied.

"Yeah, there's something I wanna go see outside." I began to put on my shoes, sitting down on the ground to do so.

"Okay! I'll go get my shoes on!" Button raced off to her bedroom where she grabbed her favorite pink tennis shoes, the kind that lit up whenever she walked. I was amazed the batteries hadn't run out on those things given the wear and tear she must've done on them in their short lives. When she first got them, she would show every neighbor on this floor of our apartment building while they watched with a fascination that matched their attitude with living in these facilities. Those attitudes were like dreams of owning a home.

Once she got them on we were off and out the door that I had forgotten to lock.

It must have only been about ninety degrees outside but without any clouds around it felt closer to a thousand. A thick bead of sweat formed on my forehead almost as soon as our feet reached the bottom of the staircase. I felt really bent out of shape and Button's energetic exuberance was only making it worse. Due to my thin frame and miniscule muscles, I always preferred hobbies that required thinking as opposed to anything that required me to move. That was probably going to be the most sun I had seen since the break has started.

The Balloon in the Storm

The wheels in my brain started turning as I kept creating various scenarios for the reasons behind the couch's obscure location. Button kept herself entertained throughout the walk by asking questions that I had no answer to. That wasn't enough though to make her stop talking so she continued on.

When we finally reached the couch, I felt my jaw hanging wide open. I could never think of any words to fully describe the way it made me feel up close. It was like a cross between saying goodbye to a friend and feeling stuck running on a wheel. Those words felt close, but they don't paint the full picture. The couch was made of a pristine blue fabric that contained the power to lull its onlookers to an encompassing nap. A light golden embroidery was implanted onto the arms with darker golden studs pierced into the couch in patterns that aligned with the stitching. There was only one pillow in the middle center of the couch that perched itself against the back and middle cushion of the couch. A bit of stuffing was coming out of the pillow which seemed out of place with the condition of the couch itself. There were also words stitched onto the pillow:

Do not sit on couch, or else

That same uneasy feeling from earlier crept its way into my body yet again. This time I was not able to hold myself to a dry heave. I knelt against the ground, my breaths staggered as I shook my head to recover. I lifted my head up a little bit and saw Button lean in closer to the couch. She read the letters on the pillow. The smile she had from behind the fridge returns. She inched her tiny body closer and closer to the couch.

If I had known what was going to happen I wouldn't have gone down there, especially not with Button. I saw her make herself comfortable on the couch, but I turned away for a moment and don't know when exactly she disappeared. It didn't feel real. She was mid-sentence when she just stopped talking and was gone.

"Big Brother, what do you..." were the last words I heard from her. When the authorities arrived, they didn't dare move the couch or risk an officer touching it. But that was probably due to my account of what I told them the pillow had written on it and what it changed to.

You were warned Charlie. Poor Button.

Charlie shifts his vision to the ceiling from his therapist's couch, "I still blame myself Doc." He reaches inside his pant pocket and pulls out a baby blue button. The therapist notes that Charlie throws the button up and down in an intentionally timed manner.

"Why is that Charlie?" the therapist straightens herself up in her chair.

"Why?" Charlie grabs the button out of the air and turns, "I lost Button and my mom 5 years ago today."

"I hadn't realized your mom passed as well Charlie..."

"She didn't," Charlie returns to tossing the button, refocusing his eyes solely on it. "She just stopped speaking to me. She blamed me for it all."

"That sounds unfair, how did you two continue living together without communicating?" Charlie doesn't respond as he zeroes in on the button toss. There seem to be unbreakable chains between Charlie's eyes and the button. Though she doesn't show it the therapist even starts to feel a bit unnerved by Charlie's metronomic timing of the toss. She clears her throat to recapture his attention. "Charlie did you not want to meet today?" He grabs the button out of the air again.

"She sent me to live with my dad." Charlie closes his eyes, "What if all of it was because I wanted to see that extravagant couch? I chose to indulge in my curiosity of it and I feel like that's why she's gone."

"Charlie, I want to be clear, the authorities conducted their investigation. It was never your fault, no one could have predicted anything with that couch. What happened that day was an anomaly."

"I should have kept a better eye on her, I shouldn't have looked away from her even for a second." The therapist notes something else in her journal. "I know carrying around one of her old buttons seems crazy... but it makes me feel like I'll never forget her."

"You're not crazy, Charlie. We all need a crutch sometimes."

"I just wish I could let her know, that I wouldn't have traded her for any type of luxury this world has to offer." Charlie closes his eyes and flips the button in the air. When it lands safely in his hand, he knows he'll never forget about his favorite Button.

Alan J. Chambers

IF I MET YOU FIRST (THE DIRECTOR)

Jack's lanky fingers meander through the auburn forest that lay above his head as he looks out across the empty parking lot. The lights that hang over the lot become more defined as his concentration intensifies with each puff of smoke he draws from his cigarette. He closes his eyes as he lays across the backside of his sky-blue car. He thinks of how the days seem to drag on, while the nights will just never quite stay.

"I hate this job," he mutters under his breath that smells of tar and coffee. His eyes strain as the "OPEN" neon sign flickers over the door of the gas station. He notices a figure of a man shift inside from the other side of the station, as his coworker, Drew, looks up for a moment before sinking back into his chair. The figure opens the fridge and grabs at a bottle of water, though he struggles as if it were a fish trying to escape his grasp. His knees buckle as he stumbles to the register. The bottle slips from his grasp, spinning and finding its way to Drew. Drew acts on a delay before he arises from his chair to assist the fallen man. The man doesn't move from the floor, staring at the ground with a blank expression on his face. Drew begins to motion toward the man though he has his hand in front of him, not to assist him up, but as if he's worried of the possible actions of the stranger. The man surges back to consciousness as if he were frozen moments before, as he proceeds to stand up.

Drew's eyes droop as he mouths the words "Are you alright", to which the man shows no form of response. The man drops a collection of quarters on the register before swiping the water bottle out of Drew's hands. Drew's eyebrows rise as a light confusion takes a hold of his face. The man proceeds to walk out of the gas station in the same direction as Jack. Jack cocks his head in the other direction to act as if he hadn't just watched the strange scene in the gas station. The footsteps of the man continue to pitter patter towards Jack, until they stop and Jack can feel the presence of the man bearing down on him like a thunderstorm.

"She's gone" the man says.

His words pierce at Jack's ears like nails on a chalkboard. The texture of his voice holds a delicate hurt that seems as if it is wrapped in glass.

"She's not coming back" his fingers tighten around the water bottle like a child's fist would wrap around a blanket. "I thought I could fix her, but I couldn't. She was always so scared of me leaving that I never realized she could"

Jack's words don't leave his mouth as the unprovoked emotion paralyzes him "I'm sorry..."

"CUT!" the director flails himself out of his chair approaching with an arrogant presence as he shadows over Liam, the actor playing the mysterious man, "You're not capturing the emotion"

The director's breaths are the only thing breaking the silence as the cast's eyes peer through the set, watching like prey in the night.

"Are you really this dumb? Do you not understand the depth of the emotion you're supposed to be conveying?" the director asks, though the unwavering gaze in his eyes is not eliciting a response from Liam.

"What are you talking about?" Drew says "I was literally speechless from the emotion he was conveying in..."

"Shut the hell up" the director responds as his eyes remain fixed on Liam, now only inches away from his face. "You're not giving me enough, Liam."

Liam's eyes dart from left to right as the director's stare suffocates him, and his eyes redden as if steam is rising to his face. It appears as if the director isn't even breathing as his constant gaze beats against the lens of his eyes.

"You're not doing enough for her. This isn't good enough for her. She needs more..." the director whispers

"Her—the scene—what... what are you even talking about?" Liam says, as he steps backwards to give himself a bit of distance.

"You don't understand. She's gone. She's never coming back." The director's intensity flashes off as if someone switched a flip inside. "She's gone," his gaze breaks as he sinks to the ground quicker than cheap fireworks on Fourth of July.

"Terrance—" Liam steps toward the director with his arm reaching for his shoulder.

"She's GONE!" the words boom out of the director's throat, each letter a piece of shrapnel roaring out of a shotgun to everyone around, piercing their ears.

The eyes of everyone grow weak. Liam is speechless as his mouth keeps opening and closing though there's nothing to say. The director's body shudders, and he slumps down to the ground, Liam kneels to him on the ground and holds him tight.

"I'm sorry," the director leans into Liam. No one speaks as the director lets out a sigh. "I'll be fine."

"Terrance, this feels like more than the scene."

"I just—I just wish I met her first." the director can't seem to stare anyone in the eyes.

"What? Who?"

"Rose, the one who the script is about." The director leaves Liam's grasp and they both rise. "I just wanted to capture how I feel."

An uncomfortable laugh breaks out among the crew starting with Drew, "Well you definitely showed us the feeling you want just now."

"Again, I'm sorry. Liam, I got carried away with all of this. I didn't mean to direct all of that at you..." The remaining tension on the set fizzles out as the director smiles and joins in on the light laughter. "I just don't have any good excuses."

"Terrance, I don't know who this person is or why she inspired this movie of yours. But I want you to know, I'm going to do my best to capture what you just showed us." Liam reaches out to the director's shoulders as he stares him in the eyes with a resolve that signals to Terrance that he made the right choice in the movie's protagonist.

"If it's okay with you all, now that that's off my chest," again the crew laughs, "I think we're ready to start back on the opening scene." As the director sits back into his chair he notices the air of the set feels closer to a clean hospital room after a successful surgery, than it does a studio backlot. Terrance nods his head, though not directly at anyone, as he feels a part of his heart unravel like a ball of yarn. It doesn't completely unwind, but it lets something out that is piercing the core. "ACTION!"

ONE DAY
(THE ANATOMY OF A MEMORY)

One day, she just stopped.

She stood frozen in place with her mouth agape as if she was about to utter a sentence that could flash her back into the moment. It seems like she was about to finish saying my name, "Terrance." Her voice saying my name hung in the balance of everything between my ears.

"Rose," I whispered as I clung with every atom of heat I produced to her cold, still figure. Clinging more to the belief that I would warm her out of this moment and she'd thaw enough to be alive again. My eyes circled around, spending seconds on every aspect of her as if I could memorize every single detail, stopping to scan any movement. I spent an eternity as I looked upon her face, raising my hand up to hold her beauty between my fingers. I didn't need for my eyes to be open to see her as my fingers traced along the lines of her chin. A tear had been frozen solid as I wiped the bottom of her face. As I looked to her eyes—my god her eyes—I saw an entire world that felt like a breath of fresh air. They continued to shift behind the freeze, from a cold blue to a naive green. They were only green when she cried.

Why couldn't she wake up.

As forever ended, I placed my forehead against hers. I had still felt her presence, as if the closer I pressed myself against her the more she was actually here again. I heard her voice ring between my ears, spinning trivial curiosities through my head. Her mouth hadn't moved in months though, she remained still with the same facial expression and same majestic eyes.

Her face had begun to fade when my vision blurred through the fire and the rain. The fires started with no trace of beginning as they danced around us, daring to lick upon our bodies. I became engulfed though I still couldn't warm her. The rain began without a cloud above, it showered out the fire, while the air remained thick with heat. When the storm diverted, I couldn't recognize her anymore. She continued to fade behind the blur until I walked away. I never turned back to see if she was ever gone. I had to let go of this memory.

LEARNING TO BE HAPPY

Coffee stains melt the letters underneath her mug. The newspaper tears, leaving a circular hole on the right side as she picks it back up. "Dammit!" she whispers holding it back under her breath. The ruined newspaper ad reads 'Around the B............e Find Your Dreams!'

She folds up the remainder of the newspaper into four squares, turning it into just one square, and sighs. She ponders if life is nothing more than coffee and promises with holes in them. She takes a deep breath as she realizes her life doesn't have time to search for trivial answers. She gets up from the countertop in her kitchen and grabs her plate of half a piece of toast and three-fourths of an egg, dumping it in the food-erator. The grumble of food being chopped apart keeps her tied to reality. She places her hands at the crown of her head before brushing her fingers through her hair, breathing like she's never felt air before. Maybe tomorrow will be better, the clock over her oven reads 7:30 AM. She presses her hands against the counter as the food-erator begins to chop at air and switches it off. She returns to her room to get ready for the day, "I don't want to do this anymore..."

She leaves her apartment with a foofy gray skirt on and a painted smile to match.

"Good Morning Lucy," her neighbor, Jay, repeats like clockwork with a voice that seems younger than sixty-two. She's not sure if he even cares to say hi or if his day would be crushed if he doesn't say good morning to everyone. Jay returns inside to his apartment before she can respond. Lucy's knees shiver as the wind from the closing door knocks against them. The chattering of her own teeth reminds her of childhood Halloween skeletons.

She makes her way down the stairs from her 2nd floor apartment. Her mind wanders to false dreams of her making a faster way down. She grips the guardrail tighter, self-aware of her thoughts, afraid to let go as she pauses at the top of the stairs. She runs down the stairs like batteries almost empty. She sinks into her car to get to work.

With seconds like summer to an elementary student, she finds herself climbing up to the rooftop floor of the building, each stairway feeling like it's adding a step at the top as she rounds every corner. The doorway to the outside looks foreign as she glares from four steps away. Three steps away and she wants to go back to tomorrow. Her heart is pounding. Two steps away and she stops on the step, unsure if she wants to go any further. One step away and the doorknob begins to scream at her, "OPEN ME UP." She's standing at the doorway, the doorknob, within reach, still taunting her. She reaches out. Her fingers taste the false hopes of copper wanting to be gold. She forces her lips to match the smile she painted on as she twists.

A crowd erupts into applause as she opens the door. Signs reading 'WE LOVE YOU LUCY' stream on the building next door. A crowd from the top of that roof break into applause only a few breaths after the crowd from the same building she's on.

"Thank you! Thank you!" Lucy cries as she waves at the crowd, delicate as the ballerina she wanted to be in her childhood. Her smile starts to feel real to her, Lucy isn't sure who she was this morning. Maybe this does make her happy after all, she convinces herself.

A man in the background leans over to his friend and whispers "Wow, she's so brave! What is this? Her 390th walk? Most people can't do one!" His friend nods in agreement, not willing to disagree about her bravery or agree that she should be doing this either way. Lucy makes her way to the edge of the building. The crew set up the rope this morning.

"Ladies and gentlemen!" the crowd erupts yet again as she speaks "It is I, Lucy! Today marks my 400th tightrope walk!" her arms shaping her like a curvy *t*. The crowd still won't let up, their screams an outlet.

She plugs herself in as they burst with energy "LUCY! LUCY! LUCY!" her battery is recharged. Her smile beaming brighter than the sun on ice as she picks herself up onto the ledge. She spins and curtsies at both crowds, across both buildings. "YOU CAN DO THIS LUCY!" the crowd says like a shadow, watching her every move.

Her left footstep lands onto the rope first. She feels as light as a dandelion in the wind. Fifteen feet separate her from safety. Her second foot balancing her as the rope is all that stops her from falling straight to the ground. She moves as delicate as a dancer placing each foot in front of the other. Life is beautiful this high up. Her head swifts down to the left as she sees cars and people, like toys and ants unaware of the world above them. Her smile no longer a secret, she didn't need this make-up. She laughs as she stops at the center of the rope. The echoes from the crowd surround her head like a crown. Lucy looks up to the sky above. She smiles. She takes another step. She slips. Both of her hands reach out.

Coffee stains melt the letters underneath her mug. The newspaper tearing, leaving a circular hole on the right side as she picks it back up. "No... No... No more," both of her hands shaking as she drops the newspaper. Lucy looks at the clock over her oven that reads 7:30 AM—

she stares intently until it changes to 7:31 AM which causes her to shudder. She never had watched it post-7:30 AM before. Lucy returns to her room with a light smile on her face. As she curls herself into bed a sense of relief breezes throughout the room; she's done with tightrope walking.

At the moment, Lucy feels herself slipping out of consciousness there's a series of two knocks on the door. Lucy's eyes shoot up and she waits to see if the knocker will disappear. Knock, knock. Lucy presumes whoever it is won't retire from knocking until she answers the door. As she looks through the peephole, she sees her neighbor, Jay.

Lucy contemplates opening the door or crushing his day by going back to bed before he can wish her a 'Good Morning'.

She opens the door, "Good Morning, Jay."

"Good Morning, Lucy." Jay removes his brown fedora, Lucy has never seen him without it before. "Wanted to make sure everything was okay. Missed you on my morning rounds, and you normally seem more punctual than I am in the morning! So, I just wanted to ask."

Lucy stares at the ground, unsure if anything is okay. She isn't sure what she's doing at this point— something inside tells her she's finally done with tightrope walking. But a louder voice is mocking her for not having any other plan.

"Look, I get it. Don't have to spill your heart out to a stranger, just wanted to check on my neighbor." Jay turns to leave.

"Wait!" The two remain still as snow in Alaska but Lucy doesn't know the words she wants to say.

"Yes?" Jay finally asks after Lucy's sustained silence.

"Why is it that every day you make the rounds around the apartment for your 'Good Morning' to everybody? You don't work here or anything."

"No one has ever asked me that before..." Jay's smile becomes contagious to Lucy as he utters, "Thank you for that."

"Of course. I've just been curious."

"I suppose it's something that I enjoy doing and it seems to make other people happy. The world could always use a little more sunshine and a little more laughter, it's my way to pitch in."

"I think I've been spreading sunshine," Lucy pauses, "But I don't think I've been getting any back with my work."

"Well, it's okay to walk away. Sometimes we forget our smiles matter too." Lucy nods a few times in response, "Well Ms. Lucy, I hope you enjoy the rest of your day. Go make a little sunshine for yourself." The man places his fedora back on his head and makes his way to his apartment.

Lucy feels like she has direction. Unsure of where it leads, but certain it's away from what's been dragging her down.

Lucy returns inside to pack a bag and leaves out of her apartment in silence. As she closes the door she feels in control of her life. She smiles, and for the first time in a long time she feels happy as she drives away.

THE STORM

Rain is pouring down like an angry alcoholic trapped in a bar, knocking down everyone's drink in the bar to avoid a relapse. I don't know where I can go to escape it tonight. I've been pacing circles around this bus stop for an hour now, wishing I had somewhere to go. I have no home. The sound of rain filters my screams at the sky. It feels like everyone is laughing at me as the rain strikes against my skin. I just want to be left alone. A tormenting series of red and blue flash at the corner of my eye. The lights are getting closer. I turn to face the opposite direction, clasping my hands together in front of my eyes like a prayer.

"Please no..." a light trickle of tears glides down my cheeks. I feel like I'm deeper than six feet under. The police car drops into the puddle out in front of me. A tidal wave of water envelops me creating a cocoon of melancholy droplets. I try to shake off the cocoon, but I can't escape the ensuing chill. My body tenses in a shiver, though I'm grateful the police car only passed by me. An older gentleman in a pair of khakis and a powder blue button-up sits down on to the rain-covered bus stop bench. A few curly twists of white hair pour out along the edges of his brown fedora. He smiles at me like he doesn't want to ask what happened.

"Well, don't you look all washed up," he says, not stopping to blink. I laugh beneath my breath at the brutish slight. I had nothing to respond with to this old man's remarks. The moment grows stale as he turns away, scrunching his nose like my scent is something offensive. "Guess that's what you get for being out in weather like this." he sticks his snout up as if he didn't feel the rain tracing down it too.

"Aren't you in the rain too?" I ask while he pushes his glasses closer to his face.

"Not for as long as you" he says while still staring off into the distance. I feel frozen but not from the rain. I bargain with my mind that he doesn't realize I'm trapped out here tonight. "Reckon you'll be out here all night?" his words still not missing a beat. I feel myself crumble underneath the weight of the storm. I don't want to do this anymore.

"What if it never stops raining" I drop down to my knees. I push my face closer to the pavement as I look at it like a reflection with my arms and legs stretched within the square of the sidewalk.

"And what if it does?" the old man, refusing to look at me, answers. "The point is, either way, you're going to get up, like them," his finger shaking as it finds its way to a red dot floating through the sky. A seed of hope is planted within me as the red dot flashes across my vision, and I feel myself starting to smile. Not sure the last time I felt that against my face. I remember as the little red dot passes, that I used to think that rain is like everyone's little happy laughs.

The dot now passed, was a big red balloon.

book iii - other conversations with myself

the other conversations

i.   a brighter morning

ii.   born mute/locks on the door

iii.   a rose

iv.   born poor/shackles on the floor

v.   a different flower

vi.   a home

conversation i.

a brighter morning

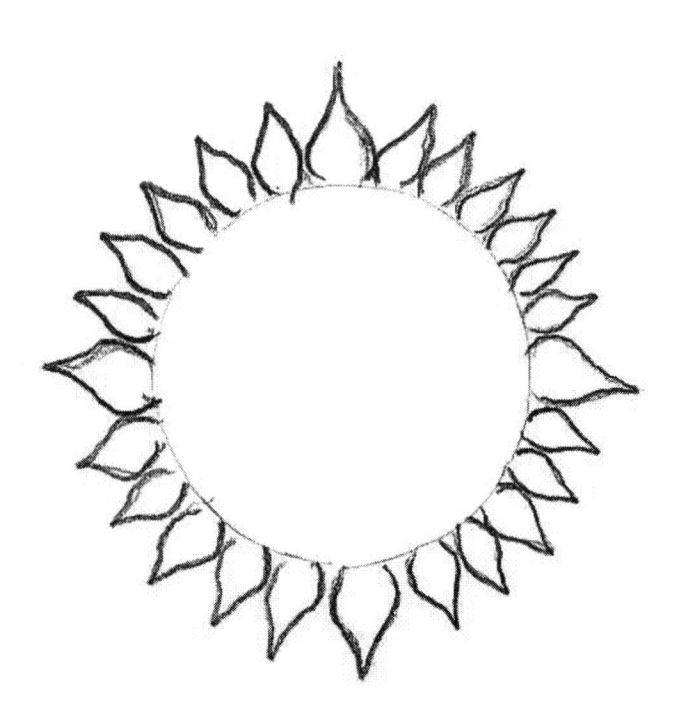

Alan J. Chambers

milk and honey

"How about that Milk and Honey"

on the counter
Feel that calm sinking into my
skin

It's like a cool Jazz
slipping off the window sill

Strange, yet refreshing

Slinking through my ear buds
making me tap
my feet

1, 2
3, 4

Entered a rhythm
I don't want to
leave

Happy
like I'm wrapped up in a blanket
I call childhood

I hope you find
Milk and Honey too

i feel okay on monday
(part iii - enfp + intj)

Cough it out.
Today feels okay.

Overcast, begins to drizzle down on the park.
A team of ducks are quacking and waddling
near the pond,
their tone makes him feel the same as
a stranger's smile
on a subway does.

A man in a light olive-green t-shirt
bends his knees,
to stand up from the outskirts
of the pond.
He smiles
as he stares up to face
the clouds and feel the
light rain against his cheeks.

Fifty steps to the bus stop,
a woman with a red umbrella
to his left.
His heart begins to sing
like a drum.
The girl from the bar,
two nights
ago.

Been blurring lines against
any other chests?
"Oh God..."

Red lines the
frame of her
smile.

I'm Joel
"My name's Carol"

They stand
closer.
Together.
Underneath her red umbrella.

They miss the bus.
Together.

weekends (ukulele)

On the weekends we all melt
into little
puddles of comfort.

colors

My brother is an artist
        I want to be the same,
though the grip of the brush
        never feels quite right

The impression of steel
        leaves marks on my fingertips
            as I paint
                music.

The G sets the backdrop
        in a lavish purple,
a quick jump to C makes
        me feel a summer day green

I can see
        why he loves this
            though my sounds are sights
                and I swirl them as so

The tempo slows. A bird begins
        floating between the colors
climbing higher and higher
        until we draw a bridge.

An E seeps onto the canvas
        a rainy gray,
            though I trickle in some D
                to lighten it with a blue like-rain.

The chorus rings. The bird maneuvers
        around the colors like water in the ocean.
Everything fits,
        I am an artist, too.

smile

Don't ever try to be
happy.

Just be your favorite

    YOU

that you can paint
in your head.

The happy
follows.

empty piano

A fake white rose sits on an empty piano.
A blind man sits in front,
with fingers still sensing the keys.
Nothing pressed.

The piano's insides are bare,
no dampers or hammers to fill the room.
An empty wooden frame,
full of dreams.

Life feels better in the dark,
he presses down on the keys.
The sound of wooden vibrations,
ivory & spruce alone.
Ticks & thocks
chopping at the air.
Never sounded so beautiful.

I sat and watched him for hours.
Thank you,
for letting me see your world.
No one can play it
quite like you do.

conversation ii.

born mute/locks on the door

born mute

There's sand in the hallway.
Dripping from my skin yet filling me.

I can't open my mouth.
It is full, yet dragging me
behind.

A hall full of color,
my mouth makes it gray.
Simple syllables sitting idly
along each childhood frame,
they won't stop laughing at me.

The sound of a choke almost
escapes from this rope I call
a tongue. Needing to scream
for a mother.
No one can
hear me here.

Tears begin to
fill the hallway.
Meshing with the sand,
into a waste of mud.
Now as clunky
as the words
that can't leave
my mouth.

Trapped in a world of
self-expression,
with a broken microphone
to spill my heart into.

The mud is coating
my throat.

Mother,
I'm begging you,
please help me.

overthinking
(among other reasons why i don't have a date this friday)

I like the way her brow furrows
when I say something provocative
The way she responds makes me
        feel like noodles
recently strained

Isn't it strange?
How a minor bump to her voice
makes me look closer at her

A bump?
Yeah, she changed the texture
of her words

Did no one else notice?
        No, it's always
just me who does

'Ask her out'
Echoes throughout the
entirety of my skull

I can't

My eyes flare
as I reflect over my thoughts
all while staring at her

I don't wanna become a dic-
A dic-
Addicted to her

The Balloon in the Storm

The nerves have started
making my bones jangle
like coins tottering down a lonely street.

The jangles make their way to my mouth
Making my teeth chatter
I fear my tongue getting caught in between

I don't speak
as she waits for me to say something else

'Say something, anything!'

My awkward stare lingers
as I take my chance for ransom
Holding it at gunpoint

    Bang
    Bang
I killed the moment

'What have you done'

I didn't wanna become a dic-
A dic-
Addicted to her

She walks out the door
I try to find the words to make her stay
Out comes an untidy mix
of letters that don't form words

But I want to see her brow furrow
and piss her off with the things I'll say
I want to hear her respond
and laugh
As I try to impress

I see her
everywhere I go.
She's with me in my mind

we've been to Paris,
Italy,
and even Jamaica

'Chase after her'
Rings through my ears
Repeatedly

I can't

My feet don't
move like I'm
bolted to the ground

I'm already a dic-
A dic-
Addicted to her

'I hate... I hate this stutter!'

She's gone
I didn't follow her
      She's gone

I just wanted to make her brow furrow

alone on a shelf

It would never be my bed she left.
    Would I want her there anyway?

She could take me to hers with ease
    I'd know her,
        remember her

To her I'll be the remnants
        of a history class

    Skimmed through.
Page after page merely grazed,

My life's stories to be returned
like a dingy school book,
sent back to the library
for some new unexpecting soul.

I'll be picked up,
    thrown aside,
        and gone again.
Back to where I belong

alone on a shelf

family traditions

At only six, he believed
he did something to provoke her.

Be a good boy

    The water runs over his
Hands.
He soaks repeatedly,
as if the cockroaches didn't live in the walls
but in his skin.
They don't go away.

Mother is trapped in her room
getting high.
He can't be like her
    Be a good boy

    Father's in a different city
he left,
but he needs him
like a beggar with outstretched arms
craving to fill the empty pit in his stomach,

Brother leaves him alone
returns home after dawn.
He can't be like him
    Be a good boy

    He stops the water pouring
Out,
He breathes in rhythm
1, - 2, - 3, - 4
To the cold grip of an obsession
He must stay in pattern

He was so young with a
naive and pure mind,
but he still feared karma
like an old man with bloodied hands.

    Be a good boy

Alan J. Chambers

little fat boy

My muscles have tightened
my stomach has flattened
but still, I see

    YOU

Always in my mirror

I've told you before, stop shoving
that ball of grease down your gullet
How many times, have I killed you?
Your spirit,
    your will to even breathe

My eyes are daggers

Your blood, sweat, and tears
tasted like black licorice
When I used to lick over your swollen cheeks.
I fear tasting you again

I kicked while you were down,
    while you would struggle for air
I watched as your fleshy innards swelled
like a rubber balloon about to pop

You begged on your knees
    heaving,
        wheezing,
            and sniveling,

To leave you be
But I wouldn't -
    I couldn't

The Balloon in the Storm

Not until you left me alone
But still
      I see you...
           salivating over my self-confidence
                craving for it like a decadent hazel cream

I want you out of my life
but you never leave,

Little fat boy
Please stop staring
      back through the mirror

intj (thoughts on life)

Everything in life is an equation

I just want to know (wh)y

bars

I didn't want to look
alone,
so, I sit at a table for
two.

But no one will come.

When did I miss the
point
in my life, when everybody else wasn't
alone?

The girl in the front of the bar
flips her hair behind her left shoulder
as her fingers circle around a glass of
Tonic & Ciroc.

Her eyes are locked into the
perfect sculpture of a
man.
His chiseled jawline
continues to
gab
up and down
up and down.
Showcasing the art of
seduction.

Why couldn't I do
that?

A group of
eleven

walks through the front doors
six guys
and five girls.

The last man stumbles his way to the bartender.
He wishes for a drink,
pointing with his eyes
to an area behind her.
He tried to ask with
words but they were
clumsier than his feet.

As he finally hits the
floor,
his friends carry him out.

I don't know
why
I came here anymore.

I feel so
alone,
as I sit as this table for
two.

intj (conversations with myself)

No one could hear
me back then.

I wanted to get away to another mind,
another voice
box. That would have felt like a
different universe.

One that doesn't
feel like an empty
squeezed grape juice
box.

Growing up would have been
a contrast. Hide and seek
would have been much more
difficult. Mom's hope
of knowing where I ventured,
between the trees
and scattered throughout my dreams,
forever altered.

Maybe it's okay.

That no one could hear
me back then.

conversation iii.

a rose

Alan J. Chambers

honey (let's be alone together)

Her hair is curly and frazzled
like bees defending their
honey, the color of her hair.
She continues to drag me
forward, by the hand.

I only notice the green of the
grass in the park, as it scuffs the
whites of my sneakers.
She tells me how she used to
come here, as a little girl.

I imagine her pigtails, bouncing
up and down
as she chases after the kites,
daydreaming that she could fly
with them

She floats between the kites
like a little baby bird in my head.
"Are you paying attention"
I wasn't. She was distracting me.

I couldn't hear the sounds of
anything else in the park
I knew the birds were chirping,
        the adults hustling,
            and the wind whistling.

They all remained muted,
and I could only hear her voice.
It was haunting
like watching a childhood video
in slow motion.

I don't remember sitting against this tree

but I remain calm
as her voice keeps ringing
a sweet melody
through my ears.

Everything is black,
but I still hear her speaking.
I'm not sure anything else is here
but me and her.
She consumes me.

scooter

Falling for her is like
us riding on my scooter.

Awkward,
there's not enough space,
and we're moving so slow.

I love every moment of it.

We ride up and down
my neighborhood,
she grins and squeezes tighter
around my stomach as the cars
behind us blast their horns.

I don't care what they do or
scream at us.
As long as she's still right behind me.

She breathes softly into
my ears,
I look back and ask

Are you okay?

It's all I worry about.
She gets the helmet,
even if I only have one.

We pull back into my driveway.
I park,
she doesn't get off.
She isn't ready to let go

neither am I.

rose's depression

"I don't have a balloon in my storm"
It's there, you just have to look for it.

She kicks up on the swings.

"No, mine got popped"
...

I stare down at the ground.

"What?"
I swear to you, you'll find it.

She stares over at me.

"Okay? So what, are you supposed to be my 'Balloon in the Storm'?"
Do you want me to be?

I look back at her.

"I don't know, whatever"
I'm sorry, I wish I could just make you understand it.

My heart sinks to the bottom of the sandbox.

"Well, what's your balloon?"
You.

She jumps off the swings and walks away.

paint

Sadness
is watching paint
drip its color off
of a canvas, after
you've lost your brushes.

Depression
is not wanting
to recreate it.

empty

Deeper.

Sink.

It feels like my chest has been
cracked open with a crowbar,
like I'm a car waiting for
service at the local auto shop,
until her, a silhouette of a broken human
wanted something else than to
feel so empty.

A smile peers through the darkness,
it seems as if she hasn't touched joy in years.
She wants more,
biting at my ear,
I can't help but feel an arousal.
I hear a moan,
not sure if it was mine or hers.

I feel detached as I realize she is
just putting on an act.
I had felt intertwined with the flow
of her, still the silhouette, until then.
She feels nothing,
I am a face in her cycle.

I don't want to be inside of her
if she'll still feel empty.

Alan J. Chambers

elevator

Up and down
Up and down
I have a moderate distaste for your emotions
You have a disproportionate distaste for my opinion

I don't know where we're going
That's okay with
me (maybe not)
You're upset with me being okay with you
not deciding

I never cared much for the destination
I just enjoyed your company
I don't think you'd say the same

You're the time of my life
I'm a strange part of
yours

Up and down
Up and down
That hurts and I bleed too
But I'll lie to keep you happy
Though you're something short of that

I stopped writing when I met you
I've never been much for talking
But you left me feeling whatever is speechless
for writing
You never could think of a certain three about me
Did you ever
love me back?

I'll never forget the first time I saw you
pass me by

The Balloon in the Storm

Cute face.
Cute nose.
Cute glasses.

You didn't notice me that day
I don't know if you have since either

Up and down
Up and down
I don't want to get off
But I think I'm starting to realize
You never got on

Up and down
Up and down

seatbelts

Flashback to a seat belt

I had to make sure hers
was on.
I can't drive without it,
      or without her.
She asked me to take her
      with me forever.

My hands grasp her
gentle fingers,
I kiss slowly as I bring the back
of her hands to my lips.

One day she'd turn
bitter towards me.
But in memories,
she remains delicate like
laces on pink ballerina shoes.

Tender is the music
as it bounces like
      vibrations
transmitted through tin cans
      to our ears.

She smiles and sways-
she doesn't dance for
      anyone else.
At least that's what she tells
me.

I can't look at seatbelts
anymore.

clothes in a cabin

Am I just a winter coat you
left hanging in a cabin
you never
intended
to go
back
to.

grapefruit (strands of her hair)

Laying about
and around.

Tangled in between
dressers,
sweltering bed sheets,
bobby pins,
soft cotton t-shirts,
TV remotes,
yesterday's fuzzy socks,
couch cushions,
and my frazzled heart.

I used to peel
them. The way a man would
peel the skin
of a grapefruit.
Waiting to feel refreshed.

Single blonde strands,
convincing me of false promises.
This will last forever.

When she left,
I found them scattered in my
apartment and mind.

I peeled them like a
grave digger,
desperate at midnight.

Free me of my sins!

One day, much like her,
those strands all disappeared,
the carcass of the grapefruit
dried out and buried.

thorns (the last rose)

cauterized wounds
along my palms,
from your love
i didn't want to let go
of.

you were a rose,
that needed time to heal.
i got caught holding onto a crumbling stem
watching your petals fall.

you needed someone
else to shatter.
to ease the pain
of a broken marriage.

i hope though
your next love helps you bloom
to be who you were meant to be.

i hope you're happy

intj (i don't know if birds laugh)

Sometimes when I look to the sky
I feel the way my heart still drops
when I think of charlatan blondes
and thick-rimmed glasses,

let's me know that I miss her
at least for a minute.

I reflect on the tension in my
teeth, as I bite my tongue
trying to hinder the memory of her
before it comes out of my mouth
like tar,
splattering on everyone around.

It was a summer in hell,
but mainly because of
unpaid electric bills.

Sweltering bed sheets and a mistress.

That's backwards in ways
but none of it was real in her
mind anyway.

The taste of powder stains
my memories' lips.
I wanted to wipe away all that
hid her.

The only scene I can never delete,
as she watches me. Watching her,
lost in her seas of ever-changing
blues and greens.

The Balloon in the Storm

While she entrenched herself in my
      eyes,
boring pools of toilet droppings.

She laughed, and for once
she actually meant it.

I hope the birds laugh too.

arrows

The only way to move forward— is to let go.

conversation iv.
born poor/shackles on the floor

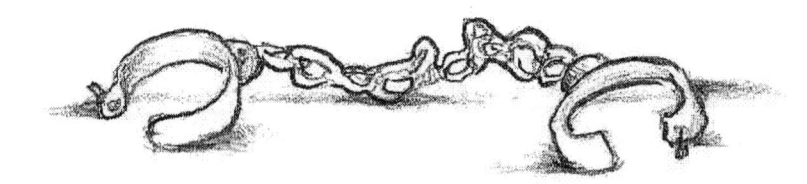

Alan J. Chambers

born poor

Sometimes it seems like there are
no short and easy metaphors
to describe how empty
poverty feels.

the wars at home

Golden rays poked holes through the unspoiled foliage;
the morning has broken out of the shackles of night.
The struggle was fierce as they fought for control over the skies,
      While I watched idly underneath
The stars fired shots, back and forth, all night to no avail-
when dawn broke the sun still rose.

The moon remained while the family of stars disappeared;
they abandoned the smallest of their kin.
He remained as I remained,
Him, tethered to the sky
I, cemented to the ground.

The midnight cold had been forgiving,
as I trudged outside earlier, through the cover of dark.
I could no longer remain in the crossfires inside,
      So here I sat
to watch a different fight.

I laid back onto the cool morning ground
still staring
at the moon.
Him
at me
      I didn't feel alone.

twenty-1/lost

Ahhh summertime
with your golden clichés and brazen fabrication

An indie record plays from the front car speakers
sounding like something old or maybe
undiscovered that strives to be vintage,
as we cruise down Menaul Boulevard
cool as a sailboat on a lazy river.

The car reeks of day old
bourbon & cigarettes
The entire car wearing sunglasses
to hide from the spirits of last night
as the sun riles them up.

The broken A/C makes me sweat
more than my sins and stories

My lover leans against me
in the back seat. She's asleep,
her breathing is soft like a cloud
that I want to fall through
again & again.

She doesn't believe in God
but she believes in me.
I don't think it's enough.
I nibble on my thumb
as I look out the window

Ahhh summertime
will I miss you tomorrow?

my father's diamonds (a text to dad)

The places you have gone,
the colors you have seen,
won't you paint me a picture so vividly.

Tell me of the cities
and their early morning horizons,
or perhaps the late night starlight

Have you found a diamond in the sky?
Show her here
      Show her here...

Does she dazzle to your eyes?
With a gentle sparkle
that puts you at ease-

I haven't found one yet;
but I can tell you of cities
where your boy has dreamt

      Oh the places you have gone,
the colors you have seen

I only wish that you could've taken me

forty-2/fear

I never thought I'd be an orphan at 42-
it feels like being stranded on a deserted freeway.
An Arizona sun beating me down with a red whip,
I stand there not knowing why or how.

I never thought I'd feel this alone at 42-
my mother had us and her parents at this point
in her life.
I have a lousy apartment with a pool on the ground floor
filled with underage drinkers
in my life.
No one knows my name.

I never thought I'd feel so dead at 42-
my father was on his third marriage
when he was this age.
I have a freezer full of three-day-old
eggplant.

I never thought I'd be so lost at 42.

intj (lightskin)

I've never known who I'm supposed to sit with at lunch.

My mind drifts down the hallways
I've walked in my life,
as the barber swivels
the chair around.

"What can I do you, man?"
Hit me with that ball fade, short.

Half-black,
half-hispanic.
Always caught between an afro and a frazzled tangle.
The razor buzz erasing it all.
The vibrations bouncing against the back of my head,
pushing me into another self.

"You sure you want it all off?"
Yes.

It's not like you're really black though right?
I'm not. I'm both.
What you know 'bout that Latin flavor then?
Poquito, but I'll still speak it
cause it's in my blood,
coursing through my streams.

"Last chance man, the top's about to come off."
Do it my man.

My identity hits the ground.
Yet,
I'm still me.
Cleans me up, that blade making me new,
as it wipes away the remainder of who I'm told I am.

Alan J. Chambers

"Alright man, $20 is your damage."
Bet.

I smile,
staring at the barber's mirrors.
Tomorrow,
I'll sit with everyone
at lunch.

what's a boat to a bed

"I bought a boat this weekend"
I just bought my first bed...

The thwap of driver meeting
golf ball, hits like
good morning.
You know you're awake.
The morning dew
stops being wet and curls
as the awkward sticks
to the ground
around us.

"...I don't know what to say to that..."
But I don't know how to feel about it...

I cried for 10 minutes after I got it,
every morning,
for a week.
It wasn't a hand-me-down,
that someone else's
Mom. Got. Me.
At a stranger's garage sale.

It was mine.

Eyes shift like
discomfort is a stench, as I place my
tee in the ground.

The club hangs over
my back, as I decide on my next
swing.

"..."

This bed makes my life
feel like a dream.

Thwap.

intj (thug life)

"You're the definition of thug life"
No, I'm not.

"No like genuinely you are"

A nerve is struck, a small twitch in my right eye,
and my heart hides, tucked between my lungs.
I've been running, my feet ache and my skin cracks.

From or to?
Maybe a bit of both,
head to the ground
so, they keep their triggers the same.

Little poor boy, big platinum dreams.

Rusted wheels moved me forward,
even when they couldn't move mom's home.
Couldn't afford it anyways.

I've spent my entire life making sure I'm not.
"I didn't say you were a thug, I said *'thug life'*"
Lost.

"In spite of all that has been thrown at you, you've persevered and gotten yourself to a better place for someone who's had every reason to fail, you never quit"

I hope I inspire your sons

"I hope you inspire the world" - Sister

blur

My heart aches for
the people I've never known,
yet always will
from my memories.

intj (homeless to the hamptons at twenty)

Melon and coconut
scents linger throughout this apartment;
    life has never smelt this good before.

I can't shake the
feeling, that I don't deserve
    a life like this.

I stare into the apartment pool,
it yearns for a name like mine.
To taste
    to feel
        to live.

Do you know what it's like to achieve your
biggest life dreams at 20?

    Inadequate.

A crystal-like cascade shapes to my body
as I dive into the pool.
I can't look back from here,
    and I don't want to.
My tears blend with the chlorine,
letting me lie to the world up above.

I quiver while the oxygen
escapes from my nostrils leaving
small bubbles to guide me
    back to my new life.

I didn't know I was allowed to be this happy

conversation v.

a different flower

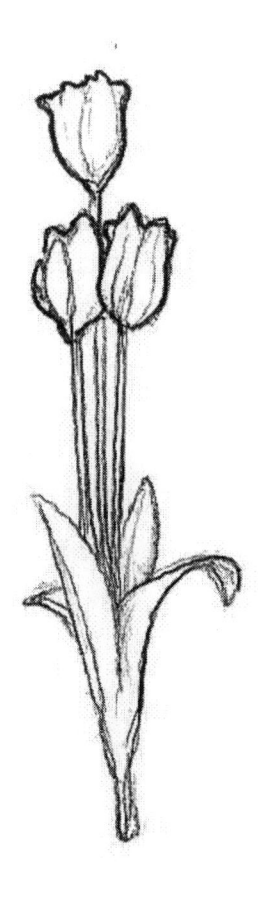

daisy

Her fingers are lax against my
chest. As I brush her shoulders,
I fear a thorn
but her stalk is bare.

At ease, but I can't help
feeling
like something is
missing.

I want to melt
in between
this doorframe
and drift to a different dream.

I'm sorry Daisy,
but maybe,
we're just not great
for the other's sake.

My fingers ease, but still
grasp around her spine
as we both contemplate
letting the other go.

I watch as she
walks to her car.
I think we both know.
She's not the one.

texting kind of love

Oops. I wrote you a love song.
But,
I forgot to hit send.

Everything could change about
us. In the next twenty minutes.
Maybe we can grab that
cup of nitro brewed coffee.
It will blow your
mind. Don't know why that's what
I'm promising you,
but opening with a
'Hi'
isn't really my style,
with you.
Or maybe we'll both go home tonight, and feel
alone.
I hope you find something to smile
about, while the nighttime traffic
burns your eyes. Wishing you were anywhere
in the distance, hiking with me like
we're each other's greatest
adventures.
Or maybe TV static will make you
smile tonight. Lovers
or strangers,
we're close to blurring the line.

But,
I forgot to hit send.

linen (my shivers)

reeling me in upon her spool.

Bind off

My words she winds like a single strand,
tangled.

Her pattern
is off, rushed

I don't want to play her game

Like a black widow
gliding along the strings she's spread
I'm merely
a pest.

Not quite afraid, as
she sets her eyes upon a
more decadent taste.
I'm not bitter.

I hope he's poison.
As he waits,
maybe he's not the one who's caught
in her thread.

But I am.

Cast on

when i first saw you (the root of a tulip)

The memory is like a
selfish ghost.
Haunting the same spot
in my brain.
It makes me smile.

Your aura is
soft,
your laugh is
not.

Did you notice my heart
as it exploded?
Fireworks throughout the
inside.
Kissing the skyline
of my smile,
an honest line
most never see.

I wasn't sure if I
held your hand
for too long.
Or if you even
minded
that I did.

"There's other people you need to meet today"
No,
there really aren't.

You're the last person I could ever meet.
And I'd repeat the same day,
the same moment,
on an endless loop
like a child's racetrack,

for you.

You could trap me in a dream,
and I'd never want to leave that bed.

Why?
Because I've known this about you, from
when I first saw you.

fleece (my fantasy)

her fingers weave dreams.

Cast on

She took my words,
and wraps us up.

I continue feeding
her thread. Like a
silver tongue but
she makes it gold.

Her eyes fixate on
every stitch. She
sees where each
single piece blends.

Each bind growing
stronger, wound
like her favorite
novel. Comforts.

I drift along, while
laying still. My mind
lost to waves. While
firmly in her lap.

I want to brew you
coffee, when you
wake tomorrow.
For my dreams.

Until then, wrap us
together in fleece.

Bind off

strange thumbs

She has some beautiful thumbs,
like they've been smashed
in a car.

Maybe more than once.

And yet,
she could wrap me round
and around
and round
that club-like digit.
Wrapped like
seconds to a
clock.

She's lost dreams of hitchhiking
the southwest,
but I will rekindle those hopes
with my hitchhiker thumb bent back.
Let's roll through tumbleweed
and coyote dust,
underneath purple skies & stars.

My God, I gotta
thank who ever smashed
those thumbs.

intj (self-conscious)

What if she doesn't like me.

What if she doesn't like
the way I write
about life.

What if she doesn't like
the way my body shakes
when my ideas zoom me through the universe.

What if she doesn't like
the town I claim
as home.

What if she doesn't like
the way I think about
her. All the time.

What if she doesn't like
the woman I call
Mom.

What if she doesn't like
the way I furrow my
brow. To think.

What if she doesn't like
that when I think about us getting old,
that I hope we get chunky.

What if she doesn't like
the black ink
that sits on top of my heart.

What if she doesn't like
the reason I got that
black ink.

What if she doesn't like...
"What if she's the one?"

after i first saw you (when a tulip blooms)

She called me her
boyfriend, within the second
week we met.

My face looked uncomfortable,
my heart felt relieved. I didn't
know anything about her.

She wraps her left arm around my right
while guiding me
to her car.
Were we drunk?
I was,
just a little bit.

"I mean I was joking..."
About dating me? Oh, why?

I wouldn't have minded her
making future
eggshells
for me to maneuver around.
I'd become the master at
trapezing eggs,
if it meant you'd say
those words again.

My body continued to scream
at her that I had no interest.
With every subtle hint of
body language, that I wrote.
While my heart pounded against
it's caging, begging me to sit
closer to her.

I was just trying to not make it so

obvious.
The thumps were bursting out
my eardrums.
I didn't mean to completely mute
the knocks of my
heart for you.

I don't think she'll ever know
I wrote this whole book
because of her
(Well I mean like, not the
sad parts though).

intj (fire burning)

"She's going to find someone else and soon"
Good

"Good?"
Yes, I'm not ready
for her. And I hope
it's someone who
makes her
laugh.

"No one's ever ready"
I'm not ready to stop
sprinting through life
yet though.

She'd make me stop,
and melt along any sidewalk
to just be a puddle she'd
pass by. The flowers would
smell nice though
that way.

"It's just a date"
But I know how I feel
about her. And that
terrifies me
because
I don't know how to feel
this way, because
     no
          one
               else
                    can
                          make me feel that way.

"Why?"

Because she makes every plan
I've ever made
fall apart,
chipping like an aged
building. Beautiful like
flower bouquets in bloom
yet, in need
of water.

"She doesn't need you to do that"
But I would.
I wouldn't need an empire,
to know I have my
Queen.

"She's just a person"
But she's so much
more.
And I cannot control that.

My world has always
been a series of Xs and Ys,
but with her,
everything just equals
out to two.

And I can't figure out how.

She's shown me the math
but what it all bubbles down
to is she changes the equations
I wrote for my life.

books

I wish my spine
was as steady
as the books
she's placed
between
my
hands

lasagna

Just talk to her.

Communicate.

Peel back these layers,

and chase away the ghosts
of memories that barely
happened. Let the racetrack
stop. Start
a new loop,
this time with her.

Remember,
she could be the one.
Your insecurities don't
matter enough to stop you.

Change your posture
as you walk closer.
Let her know with your gestures,
that you think she's a
vivid dream. Speak of the
words you write,
the ones about her.

Let her build upon your
plan. Maybe she's an
architect.
Maybe even
better than you.
You can't solve all of life's equations
without her help.

Just start with something simple.
Hey... Umm... Do you like lasagna?

tulip

"I'd love lasagna!"
yesterday echoes

Shoulders twitch,
as I consider choosing
another flower.

"Red, white,
purple, or yellow?"
The female cashier stares idly at me,
as I wonder which colors
my date would like best.

Four fingers tap.
Along the service counter.
Demanding an answer.

But I can't decide so easily.
She is more to me than a
daffodil or daisy.
She is a
tulip.

Less romantic than
a rose,
but her lively petals more
vibrant.

They make me feel
brand new. Just like
she does.
She makes me feel
bloomed,
like springtime dancing.

May I have the yellow tulip, please?

summer jam (hold me close)

Knees bend, and twist,
Contorting like butter on a summer night,
soft but not melted.
        The arms flail
                but there's still a direction.

"Darlin' swing me round"
        as they spin deeper into the night.

Each step they cannot miss,
like the taps are playing notes
      on a piano.

The air has a trace of freedom,
      poppin' fireworks.

"Darlin' swing me round"
        as the band man hits a high.

Keep twirling like childhood independence.
Is that a scent of summer?
Can feel it trickling between
      little fingers,
honey and jam.
        Sweet isn't it?

"Darlin' swing me round"

      Darlin'

my hands will tremble.

sweet banana pie

"Why did you feel like
you couldn't ask me out"
My stutter only comes
out when I'm
the kinda

nervous

you make me

"I made you that
nervous though..."
You make me
mushier than

bananas

I had to fight every
impulse trampling
along my insides
to not be
sampling upon your
lips,
cause I thought
maybe you'd also get the
buzz of sound
you make me feel,
tingling along the outskirts of
my skin,
and then you'd smile
too, and say
"WOW!"

all I could manage
back then
was a smile.

intj (love & writing)

Balance
but I try to break it
with every line I (right)

That's not (write)

My mind continues to seek
a way to (peace) the
puzzles
together

The spacing keeps
changing

There is no science
to the delicate traces
she leaves
along my bones

But I'll keep trying
to find it
Until I feel (piece)

It bothers
but I feel myself
growing

a better botanist

He picked up the
flower
I liked most.

The fantasy of us,
wrapped together in fleece
unraveled, like a golden
vinyl record scratched
along the surface,
in my mind.

No midnight dances or awkward
lasagna dates
for you and me.
I'm sure I'll be fine without
the carbs.

But I know you look
happier.
And I know he makes you
laugh.

That matters more
to me.

But I hope for me.
That I'll find
a different flower.

conversation vi.

a home

bikes

Steady,
      like a slo-mo video.

I just want to be outside
with the whir of chains
and cars. These chains
free my spirit.

Smooth like a circle,
breath and legs.
In the same pace,
yet separated by
seconds. I want
to blur time to

grab the adventures
outside of walls.

Take me to a volcano
spewing its love.
Take me to a forest
with its hidden secrets.
Take me to a waterfall
where I can learn what it means to believe.

    Take me anywhere but home.

moment

Focus

Live in this moment
Stop talking to
yourself

The pin drops
sending my mind into a wave like a
palindrome

Focus

Her lips move gentle like a piano
hammer
Throwing me into action

I need to
respond
Be clever, stop thinking

Focus

With a foxlike
sneer
I glide across the keys

Hitting notes and highs I didn't
know
lived in me

Baby isn't it grand?

Focus

I'm
not the same

Not anymore

I'm
in tune with the moment

my conversations are like double dutch

The sound of rope hitting
concrete.
Makes me laugh.
I always look down to my
feet right after
I hear it.

I didn't always know how to jump in.

Feet tangling with rope
like words to a tongue.

I kept trying though.

One whole jump.
Then two.
Then three.
Then I couldn't stop.

I still sometimes forget when to jump in today
and the rope gets tangled.

But I've learned that that's okay.
I'm just happy I now know how.

.

a joy like shopping carts

A false spring cool,
    I've been here before.
This parking lot
is a little more than just nostalgia,
for a time when I was afraid of
the dark outside.

Like a bandit tearing out of the
grocery store. The clerk smirking
instead of chasing behind me.
I won't steal this cart, just the
joy it brings.
The friction of rubber
and street tar burning into pure
childhood bliss.

It feels like fresh ocean air
as the wind whips across the cart,
    singing like a voice I'd remember hearing.
While racing to the car,
    nothing can stop me here.

Mom, I'm coming home

(i made it) portugal.

The beach reminds me of
blue soap.
The one mom put in the bathroom.
When we were a
family.
Sailboats and sand
on the front
sticker.

"Why'd you come to Portugal?"
I didn't really know
anywhere else to go.

The waves come
ashore. Washing my feet,
of any aches and cracks
that came
along my path.
I feel so cleansed

"You've never had a dream vacation?"
I never thought
I'd get the
chance.

I wasn't taught to
dream as a child,
just how to survive.

I only knew
I wanted more
than that.

I sink into the sand.
Is this really my life.
The sand feels warm like a

slice of June.
Will my nightmares
ever return?

Portuguese letters and words
escape comprehension.
I like the way they say
them though. All around
me.

A family is walking their dog.
I like the way they leave
their footsteps on
the beach.

Life changes with each step,
yet somehow
it always finds the right paths.

the rest of our weeks
(part iv - intj + enfp)

It's early morning.
Sunlight beginning to peak through the
white curtains.

She's wearing my soft lilac t-shirt,
while she sleeps.
The ceiling fan no longer haunts me,
while it swings around above me.
It no longer makes me feel alone.
She clears the mist out of my life.
Everything feels clear.

In her sleep,
she still reaches for my hand.
I oblige, kissing the ring
sitting on her left hand.
Fourth finger,
inscribed with our initials
J & C.
She smiles.
I breathe.

She will always be my favorite adventure.

happy

I feel like I'm home

AFTERWORD (KINTSUGI)

Kintsugi.

An art of broken pottery where the cracks

are filled in with gold.

Writing these stories made me feel whole again.

I hope my stories and poems have given you hope to

get you through the storms in your life.

Good luck and I hope you find your balloon.

Help me make my voice loud!
If you enjoyed my book, it would help me share my story out
to others by leaving a review on Amazon for my book.
If you're interested in my upcoming books or are a student in search of a
scholarship register for Alan's Dream Scholarship at
www.alanjchambers.com for future updates!

Alan J. Chambers

ABOUT THE AUTHOR

Alan J. Chambers was born in Wyandotte MI, but raised in Albuquerque, NM. He received his Bachelor's Degree in Accounting from the University of New Mexico because of his love for language and the connections it makes, especially within the world of business. He currently resides in Northwest Arkansas working in trade in the grocery industry. He grew up playing music with friends in Albuquerque in various bands in high school; his love for writing their music transformed into a love for writing stories. His childhood mutism and speech problems are minimized and he's sprinting after his dreams. In his free time, he likes to kick back, relax, and chill by a pool in the summertime while sipping on some pink lemonade.

Made in the USA
Middletown, DE
27 October 2018